Pat MacEnulty holds a doctorate in English from the Florida State University. Her bachelor's degree is from the University of Florida. She is the recipient of an Individual Artist's Fellowship from the Florida Arts Council and several other fellowships and awards for her writing. Her novel, *Sweet Fire*, was published by Serpent's Tail.

Also by Pat MacEnulty and published by Serpent's Tail

Sweet Fire

While most people Trish's age are listening to Led Zeppelin and watching Starsky and Hutch on TV, Trish spends the 1970s stealing and cheating to score. Heroin, pharmaceuticals, whatever she can get hold of. She travels from Florida to California and Mexico, hustling all the way, and always in the company of the wrong kind of men, whom she attracts wherever she goes. There's not a rehab unit in the country that hasn't thrown her out at least once.

Far from under privileged, as the daughter of a concert violinist and a college professor and poet, it is hard to understand what set her on this self-destructive path. What in her past shaped a future of ripping off drugstores and being sent to jail?

Sweet Fire, the author's first novel, grabs you by the throat and never lets you go.

'Her lean, easy prose propels her story beyond the personal, making for more than convincing fiction' *Observer*

'[MacEnulty] writes about her subject with sympathy, wisdom and – an unexpected blessing – humour . . . Trish remains an engaging character whose innate, if often subdued, grain of goodness and interest in humanity keeps the reader on her side' *Guardian*

'An amazing view into the mind of someone driven to recklessness by unknown demons' *Venue*

'It is entirely to MacEnulty's credit that she confronts the demons head-on in a hilarious, unflinching, vital account, devoid of sentiment or platitude' *Herald*

The Language of Sharks

Stories by Pat MacEnulty

Stories have been published as follows:

"Blue Abstraction" in *Sun Dog: The Southeast Review*; "Floating on the Darkness" in *The Sun*; "The Hawk's Shadow" in *Green Hills Literary Lantern* and *Explorations*; "Like Someone in a Coma" in *Poetic Justice*; "Some Place to Live" in *Snake Nation Review*; "Singing in the Free World" in *Crescent Review*; "Fire and Light" in *The Flint Hills Review;* "The Hurricane Dance" in *Oyster Boy Review;* "Dancing for Poppa" in *AmericanWay In-flight Magazine* and *Language and Literature* (McDougal, Littell); "Giving up the Guilt" in *Main Street Rag*; "Picture Day" in *Moxie.*

Library of Congress Catalog Card Number: 2003115193

A complete catalogue record for this book can
be obtained from the British Library on request

First published in the UK in 2004 by Serpent's Tail,
4 Blackstock Mews, London N4 2BT
website: www.serpentstail.com

Printed by Mackays of Chatham, plc

10 9 8 7 6 5 4 3 2 1

CONTENTS

ACKNOWLEDGMENTS

First, I want to thank the usual suspects: Pamela Ball, Mary Jane Ryals, Kim Garcia, Lizanne Minerva and the 1995–96 Wings Workshop (Ron, Mac, George, Russ and Michael) for being great friends and exemplary writers. I am also grateful to the Florida State University Creative Writing Program for a Kingsbury Writing Fellowship and a Dissertation Fellowship. Also much thanks to the Florida Arts Council for financial support. Thanks to my outstanding editor Amy Scholder for helping me wade through the words. Finally, I want to thank my coaches over the years: Harry Crews for laying the foundation, Lynda Schor for helping me find a voice, Janet Burroway for her advice and her terrific book, the late Jerry Stern for more than I can possibly say, Les Standiford for laughter and for offering a different perspective and Sheila Ortiz Taylor for continued, unwavering support and encouragement.

In memory of
Michael William Gearhart
January 1, 1957 to Sepember 26, 1996

Blue Abstraction

In New York, where my parents met and wooed and wed, the artists slashed convention with strokes of bright greens and blues invaded by a saffron cancer, or they delved into half-worlds of brown, black and white, the tubes of paint squeezed directly onto the canvas. Everything was art. But my parents had left New York, and my mother sat at the window of a small apartment in Coconut Grove watching the cockroaches, wondering if life was worth the effort.

One muggy night, my father, the piano teacher, came home, forehead gashed and bloody. His pupil had thrown a metronome at him, he said. Mother knew the score. She bandaged him and then poured him a glass of dark German beer. It was good, cold and frothy. They put Mahler on the phonograph and sat on the living room couch, underneath the ceiling fan's breeze. He began to tell her stories of his boyhood. Her laughter rose like steam into the air, then slowly turned to water as the night grew cool.

Some time in the early morning, she said, "Are you ready for bed?" They had not kissed in months. He followed her to the room at the back of the apartment, fell with her into the bed and brushed his hand against her skin, swirled his fingers over her fine dark hair. While de Kooning worked late, creating a bright colossus of colors, letting ropes of oil paint drip from stiff brushes, one of my father's sperm permeated a seed, leaving the rest to drip along the white canvas of her thigh. Ah, but his pupil returned, and he left for good a few weeks later.

Floating on the Darkness

One summer my step-father evaporated from our lives. First, he went to a place to dry out. No one gave me the details. Then one morning he was back with us, this ghastly figure, a wasted vision of cirrhosis, wavering in the kitchen as I was hurrying out of the house, plane ticket in my hand.

"Just for a week or two, Lillian," my mother whispered as she shoved ten dollars in my hand for the cab to the airport. I crossed the porch and followed the walkway through our overgrown lawn, weedy and wild with St Augustine grass muscling through the cracks in the concrete. I wondered what mother was planning to do with him. He had seemed like such a nice guy when she married him with his big square head and crinkly eyes. I still wore the topaz earrings he had given me when they first got married.

I spent ten uneventful days making crab apple jelly with my Aunt Cleo in Rhode Island, came back home to Florida and he was gone along with my mother's bedroom furniture. My mother and I never mentioned him again except as Mistake Number Two.

"You've got a way with men," I'd say.

"Yeah, a bad way," she'd answer, with a smile bright and brittle as a Christmas ornament.

We sold the big brick house on Evergreen Avenue and moved to a brand new second-story apartment with a vaulted ceiling, a view of the swimming pool and a small canal in which other residents had tethered their yachts and outboard motor boats. My mother kept a bright yellow canoe on the lawn.

Every day when she got home from her job as the county school superintendent, my mother would drag the canoe to a ramp, nose it into the water, place one foot in and push off with the other. Then with swift, strong strokes, she'd paddle away into the water by herself. Sometimes I'd watch her from my bedroom window as she cut through the canal like a needle through a trickle of thick syrup. Every time, as she got to the wider river, she'd shrug her shoulders and toss her head as if she was squirming out of an ill-fitting dress. Then she'd disappear around the trees.

We had moved out of my high school district but since my mother was the county's Education Empress, I kept going to the same school; only now she had to drop me off in the mornings. My boyfriend Bo always brought me home, and we would spend the intervening hours between our arrival and my mother's return sliding around naked on the gold satin sheets in my bedroom.

"Have to go home and have our afternoon snack," we'd

tell our friends at school if they wondered why we didn't hang out with them at the Burger King parking lot for long.

"Bo has such an appetite," I'd say, waving as we drove off, Leon Russell's bayou voice pouring out the windows of Bo's ten-year-old Cadillac.

Bo was an artist. He drew pen and ink pictures of creatures that were part human/part shoe and flying ears with stars swirling out of them, the canal floating in space and bald-headed women and long tongues with Shakespeare's sonnets written on them. One wall of my bedroom bore his works like a private gallery. All the pictures were inscribed "To Lillian."

Bo's senior prom was held the next spring at the women's club. My mom and Rick had been married in the garden there. But that was a lifetime ago. Now I was a junior in high school, and I wore a blue dress from K-Mart with slits up to the middle of my thighs and knee-high baby blue suede boots that cost five times as much as the dress. Bo wore his black tails with a pair of jeans. We didn't dance. We just drank punch to irrigate our cottony mouths and laughed at the corsaged girls and their dates with their hopeless smiles, dancing stiffly in an awkward parody of people having fun.

"Sometimes it's so embarrassing to be white," I whispered to Bo. With our long brown hair and our anti-religious poetry published side by side in the high school literary magazine, Bo and I seemed destined to take our coupledom into college with us. After the prom about ten of us got a room at the Holiday Inn where we drank beer and smoked fat joints of Mexican Red. We went outside and shed our clothes by the pool. The water glowed turquoise and we entered slowly, dipping our bodies like pearls into the liquid. Bo's eyes slid across to me and then made a methodical check of all the other pairs of eyes to see if any one of the guys was glancing my way. They were all laughing, stoned and spitting water at each other. Except for Frankie Jacks who looked at me and said, "Smile, Godiva."

Bo snarled, and someone told him to lighten up.

I sunk down, let the water close over my head, then pushed off against the side and soared along the whole length of the pool. My mother, who had been a lifeguard as a young woman, had taught me how to swim the crawl, the backstroke, the butterfly and the breast stroke, but I always liked mermaiding underwater the best. I imagined that being naked like this must be how it felt to float in space. I loved to think about space, starlight spattered across the infinite black like a shotgun blast, the buoyancy of nothingness.

We all got out, wrapped ourselves in thick white hotel towels and packed into the room. Most of us got dressed, at least partially but one couple named Dave and Linda stretched out pale and naked as newborns on one of the double beds. Soon all the guys were nudging each other, and the other girls were all riveting their heads around. Bo and I just stared as Dave's arching back grew taut as a bow. Linda's bony legs protruded above him like the legs of a grasshopper until finally Dave collapsed, his arrow released, and Linda drew her initials in the sweat on his back. Linda was one of my best friends. I felt creepy as if I had defiled her in some way by watching. Bo laughed, but he had a strange uncertain look in his half-closed eyes and we went home early. He didn't even see me to the door when we got there, just kissed me quickly and said goodbye.

A week later, Dave, Linda, Bo and I rode over to the Burger King after school in Bo's car. I had a razor that I'd been using to splice audio tape for a school project and for some reason I still had it in my hand.

"What's 'at for?" Bo asked.

"To slit my wrists," I answered, in keeping with the morbid humor we all kept tucked in the sides of our necks like pouches of venom.

"I wish you'd succeed," he said, but the irony was noticeably lacking as he stared straight out at the road. I glanced back quickly at Dave and Linda. They found something interesting on the ceiling by the overhead light to study while I clung there to the front seat with my lips stinging, not knowing what to do with my hands, my hair suddenly feeling snaky and long and oily and everything about me suddenly too visible, too naked. I dropped the razor out the window, and it flashed as it fell to the road like a silver minnow.

Bo broke up with me that summer. He never said why, but I had a feeling it had something to do with a green-haired girl on the swim team. I cried so violently that I vomited blood. I skipped the last three days of school, stayed home and listened to my mother's old Billie Holiday records and snuck shots of whiskey out of the bottle of Chivas that she saved for special occasions. But the next weekend I surrounded my crimson eyes with thick rings of black eyeliner and blew into a keg party all by myself. The Allman Brothers were playing on the stereo. Dave and Linda were there, sitting on the couch, sharing a cigarette. Dave winked at me, and Linda gave me a frosty smile. I wandered out the back door.

Frankie Jacks with the squinty green eyes, thick rough of sandy brown hair and the thin grin had found a perch outside on the deck.

"If it isn't Godiva," he said and lit my cigarette. We stood there, looking at each other for a long time.

After our second date, Frankie and I pulled into the parking lot of the apartment complex where I lived. We'd been to see *Superfly* at the downtown movie theater, something Bo would never have dreamed of doing. I glanced through the plastic Mardi Gras beads hanging from the rearview mirror of his van, saw Bo's black caddy and said, "Oh, God."

Frankie said, "Want me to walk you to the door?"

"No, better not," I said. "Thanks for the movie." I was feeling pretty pissed because I really wanted to knock the hash pipe and the roach clips and the spare Kawasaki parts off the console between us, crawl into his lap and taste the salt on his lips for an hour or so. Instead I stepped on a copy of *High Times* lying on the floorboards and let myself out.

I walked slowly up the concrete stairs, along the balcony and then into the apartment where my mother and Bo were practically nestled on the love seat. Bo's eyes were red and biscuity, and my mother looked up at me with a helpless grimace. I pulled a Kool from my purse, lit it and sat down in the wingback across from them. I propped my feet up on the coffee table, covered with my mother's *Smithsonian* magazines. She excused herself and went upstairs to her room. We heard her TV come on.

"Lillian, is there any possibility of us ever getting back together, ever again?" he asked.

I noticed that I had a burn hole in my silk shirt, a casualty of popping seeds. I looked back up at him, blew a finger of smoke above his head and said, "I'm sorry, but no. I hope we can still be friends."

Bo wept, tears soaking his scraggly brown beard as he cursed Frankie Jacks and called him a "buddy-fucker" though they had never been buddies. He finally left, and my mother came back down as soon as the door shut. She sat down on a bar stool by the kitchen pass-through while I fixed a grilled cheese sandwich. Her hand twitched nervously on the counter.

"He was so upset," she said. "He was crying. He told me that you hitchhike."

That jackass, I thought. I flipped the sandwich over.

"Not anymore," I told her, "I gave that up a couple of years ago." This was true, but she looked away and I knew it hurt her that I had such secrets. She used to be my closest pal, and I was her one true ally. When I was little, she would swing on the swing set right beside me or play in the sandbox with me. I felt so lucky to have a mother like her – laughing and kid-like. Even now, we could spend hours in the mall shopping together and going to the ice cream place for a banana split afterwards. She went to bed that night with a worried-mother look shrouding her face like a veil.

The next week my mother and I went shopping for a car. I knew she was afraid that without Bo to chauffeur me around I'd start thumbing again. Or maybe she just wanted to show how much she trusted me. Or maybe she was just sick of sharing her own car. All I know is that she dragged me out of the apartment way too early on a Saturday morning without even a cup of coffee in either of us.

We looked at a Chevy Nova, a Ford Pinto, a few generic Buicks and Oldsmobiles, stopped for some lunch and then late in the afternoon we pulled into the Volkswagen dealership. I saw it instantly: a red Volkswagen beetle with a black top. Mom followed me over to it, and when our eyes met, we didn't have to say a word. We knew we'd found my first car. Regardless, she had to make the requisite objections.

"Can you drive a stick shift?" she asked.

"I'll learn," I said.

"It doesn't have air conditioning," she remarked. I shrugged. Then she looked at the sticker price.

"Not too high, not too low. Where's the damn

salesman?" she wondered, her purse hanging on her arm, her check-writing fingers wiggling like worms above a fishbowl.

The car was my passport. I wore it like a turtle shell. Some nights if I had nowhere to go, I'd just circle the neighborhood, shifting and downshifting dreamily. When school started back up, I drove it every day to the small white house where Frankie Jacks lived with his mother. He had a couple of morning classes at the junior college and I usually made it to my early classes at the high school, but in the afternoon, I'd spend fifth and sixth periods lying on Frankie's undulating waterbed while he played licks on his electric Fender.

Frankie was sweet, his hair was long, and he was a gazillion times more popular than Bo. I was sort of hoping that things with him would last a while.

One night around Halloween, I was sitting at home, watching a *Star Trek* rerun and drinking a glass of Diet RC Cola. Mom had made spaghetti that night, and wafts of tomato sauce and oregano swam in the air like invisible eels. She sat down beside me and put a hand on my leg. I didn't have a worry in the world except that I was vaguely wondering what Frankie Jacks was doing quote with the boys. I gazed down at her hand. The skin was slightly splotched and bunched up around the knuckles. I thought about how her hands sometimes smelled like onions and sometimes like Estee Lauder. Then the commercial was over and I turned back to the television.

"Lillian, isn't it time to start thinking about college?" Mom asked.

"Why?" I asked.

She didn't have a ready answer, but she stammered around until she found another question.

"Well, what are you planning on doing after you graduate?"

"Get a job, I guess," I said. I sucked cola from an ice cube, not wanting to disconnect my attention away from Captain Kirk and the television set long enough to deal with her. It was the episode where Ricardo Montalban is the super-hunk from the end of the 20th century. It was the forty-seventh time I had seen that particular show, but I always liked it.

"Lillian, how can you even consider not going to college?" she asked. "You've always loved books. You're a bright, very bright, girl. National Honor Society, for God's sake."

What I really wanted to do for the rest of my life was get stoned and lie around while Frankie Jacks played me like a twelve-string. Or else work on movies about outer space. My mother searched my face, looking for answers I didn't have.

"I don't want to get too smart, Mom. I don't want to end up like you," I said, looking away, trying to get out of the glare of her high beam eyes.

She didn't move for a moment, and then she stood up and walked across the living room to the front door. As she opened the door, she wheeled around, and she seemed to uncoil before me, all that tight wrapping slipping away.

"Things could have been different," she said. "He tried to kill me. Sometimes I wish he had." Then she walked out and let the door fall behind her.

Let her go, I thought. I sat there slumped into the couch for a few minutes, listening to the TV but not watching it. Maybe she wouldn't come back. People had disappeared before – my father when I was six, my step-father ten years later. Just like *Star Trek* characters dissolving into molecular patterns on the transport pad. But her words began to sink slowly through my consciousness, and before they hit bottom, I bolted up and dashed outside.

From the balcony I could see my mother's Impala in the parking lot in its usual place. I went down the stairs, two at a time and looked around the front of the building. Then I walked around back by the pool. Empty lounge chairs were clustered together as if a party had been abruptly halted. A lone raft floated on the surface of the pool. I clambered up on the diving board and looked around. Lights glowed from various apartments, but there was no visible life anywhere except for the palm trees that rustled in the autumn breeze. And then I saw movement by the canal.

I walked fast across the concrete deck around the pool, down along the thick cushion of grass by the canal. I could smell the brown water and the decay of leaves on the opposite shore. When I came up, she was dragging the canoe toward the water. She had the two paddles in one hand. She always took one as a spare in case she dropped hers.

"Who tried to kill you?" I asked as I came up.

"Who do you think?" she asked, not looking at me. She had knelt down by the canoe. I hunkered down next to her.

"Mistake Number Two?" I asked.

She nodded. "When you were in Rhode Island, he was drunk, poured gasoline on the bedroom, said he'd burn me alive. Then he started lighting matches and laughing." She paused and the palm trees rattled their long dry leaves. "I barely got away. But I did. Locked myself in the bathroom, climbed out the window, dropped to the ground from the second floor, hobbled over to the Willards' house next door and called the police."

"What'd the cops do?" I asked.

"Locked him up. That's the last thing I know about it." She rubbed the muscles of her arms. I felt hot and then cold. I remembered fights about life insurance policies and about women at our house. And I remembered that the rug and the bed were all missing from her room when I returned and the walls had been freshly painted. He had wanted to take my mother away from me, to leave me all alone. I let my fingers slide across the chrome siding on the top of the canoe. How different everything would have been. Without her. It seemed as if she had always been with me even when I was by myself, like that long cord that keeps the astronauts from floating off into oblivion when they leave the space ship.

She stood up.

"Where are you going?" I asked.

"Just out," she said. The river slithered over the land like a black water moccasin, and the sky dangled a piece of broken moon above us.

"Can I come with you?" I asked.

She handed me a paddle, and I pushed the front of the boat into the murky water.

"You'll wind up living in a trailer, married to some guy whose idea of a good time is to get his pickup truck stuck in a mud pit," she said, dragging the back half of the boat.

"Oh, I won't marry him," I said. I stepped in and positioned myself in the front.

"That's a relief," she said.

I felt my mother's weight as she got in the back.

"At least take the damned SAT," she said and threw a small rope into the bottom of the canoe.

"All right," I said. What neither of us knew was that before the school year was out, I would find myself on a path of self-destruction that would eventually bring my mother the atheist to her knees, begging God for strength. Frankie Jacks and I would discover heroin and needles, and nothing that we had loved before would matter to us for a long time. But this had not happened yet. And I suppose that is why I remember this night so clearly.

I looked around and saw her hand gripping the oar. Then she shoved off. The canoe tottered for a moment before it slid across the black water and the night folded around us.

Like Someone in a Coma

Baby oil. That's all Liz can smell anymore. Baby oil has seeped into the crevices of her palms, her cuticles, through the pores of her white and pink hands. She uses the baby oil on the backs of the men who come to see her at La Femmes Massage Parlor on Dixie Highway. She pours it across their backs: brown skins, pale white skins, some thick with muscle, others scrawny, ribs buckling through. Before she puts baby oil on them, she explains the price structure – $35 for a plain back massage, $40 for a full body massage, and $50 for half and half, which means she massages them and then they massage her.

"What do I get for a hundred bucks?" they usually ask.

"Anything you want as long as you're done in half an hour."

Liz does not think being a hooker is as bad as some

things. Her auntie teaches high school English and that is much worse than turning tricks as far as Liz can tell. She left her auntie back in Columbus, Georgia, and moved to Miami six months ago. She brought her boyfriend, Tommy, with her. While she waits for customers, she studies for her classes at the community college. The other girls at the massage parlor think she is weird.

The only time being a hooker is really a drag is when the guys who come in are young and drunk and in a pack. Then she is the sirloin in the midst of the dogs. Usually, the men come in by themselves. They are from out of town or recently divorced. Lonely. She can offer them a drink to help them relax. The drink is on the house.

Liz's favorite trick so far has been a twenty-eight-year-old virgin. Liz is only nineteen, and she looks sixteen. She has long straight brown hair that she wears in a ponytail. Her skin is clear, and except for the needle marks on her arms, she looks like the girl you wanted to take to your senior prom. When he told her he was a virgin, she smiled and took his hand. They sat down on the double bed in the little room that smelled like baby oil. She smiled sweetly and told him about being from Columbus, Georgia, and about her classes – Intro to Psychology, Business Math, Comparative Religions, American Lit.

"Can I touch your legs?" he asked.

"Sure," she said.

She even kissed him, kissed him on the neck and then on his nipples after she unbuttoned his shirt and then on his navel. She knew that he was not lying about being a virgin. He made her think of Antarctica – unspoiled landscape. Later she slid on top of him and she said, "It happens just like this." And she guided him into her. "Do you like that?" she asked.

"Yes," he said, "Yes, I do. Yes, I like that."

He was happy, and for a half an hour the two of them were sweethearts in the small baby-oil-smelling room with the red light glowing on the night stand.

When Liz is fired from the massage parlor for stealing money by a fat little man with a Brooklyn accent, she has to call Tommy from a pay phone down the street. Semi-trucks roaring by blast her with air, their headlights blaring in her eyes. Cars slow down but she waves them angrily on. She does not care much that she has lost the job. All the girls eventually get fired, because they all start keeping the house cut. They are supposed to write down every customer and slide thirty dollars from each one into a floor safe. But every once in a while, they do not write down the trick and they keep all the money. And every once in a while, the management sends in a spy.

Tommy pulls up in the big green Impala. The car is ten years old and dented on both sides, but runs good because Tommy knows everything there is to know about fixing old cars.

"That fat little fuck," Tommy says when she tells him what happened. He squeezes her thigh and tells her not to worry about it. Tommy tried to work once, but he got a terrible case of the hives, and so now his main job is to take care of Liz and her car. He fixes coffee for her every morning and runs the bath water nice and hot the way she likes it. When she comes home from work or from school, the kitchen is clean and Tommy always has a joke for her. She cannot remember him ever saying anything mean to her.

They drive down to Perrine to cop as much heroin as they can get for fifty bucks. A black man named Henry cops their dope for them in return for a cut. Henry likes Tommy a lot. Everyone does. Henry and his girlfriend have five children. They are good kids, but they do not have much room and sometimes one will sit in Liz's lap as she waits for Henry to come back with the dope. She likes the feel of their squirmy bodies in her lap and the dirty child smell emanating from their warm necks.

Tonight as they wait, Liz wants to remember something good that has happened in her life. Meeting Tommy was good, but also not so good. Tommy was the first person to bring the needle into her life like a torch into the darkness. Now sometimes she thinks it is burning her alive, but because she is so stoned she cannot tell for sure.

She thinks about her childhood, remembers Auntie tucking her in at night and reading bedtime stories to her or going to church with Auntie and playing in the warm kitchen while the ladies cooked German chocolate cakes, meringue pies and these delicious powdery white cookies with tiny pieces of nut inside. She liked to listen to the church ladies tell their stories. Everyone knew that more gossip got stirred than cake mixes, but Liz could live on those stories of ailing children and wandering wives and men who made pacts with Satan.

There is one story that Auntie told her about herself. It was the one about how Auntie had come to be her mother. It was like the story of a birth, the way it was told over and over again. Liz knows it is the story of her origin.

"I had come to Atlanta to see how your mother was faring since Harold died. I knew I should have come sooner, but just seemed like time crept up on me. By then you were already three years old and Harold got killed before you were even one. (As usual he was in the wrong place at the wrong time.) Well, the taxi cab pulls up in front of this low-class-looking clapboard house, grass needs mowing bad and already I can hear you screaming your little heart out. I tell the taxi cab driver don't even shut off the engine, and I go storming into that house. There is your mother (empty bottles of Old

Grand Dad everywhere) standing in the kitchen and she is plucking the feathers out of a poor little parakeet. And you are hiding underneath the kitchen table in nothing but your underpanties, just screaming like to bring the roof down. And the parakeet was screaming. I didn't know which one to save. Figured it better be you since you are my poor dead brother's only child. So I snatched you from under the table and took you right back outside. We got in the cab and went straight to the bus station."

"What did I wear on the bus?" Liz wanted to know.

"You wore one of my blouses that I had packed in my suitcase. It was a pretty blue-flowered pullover from J.C. Penney. And you got motion sickness on the bus and threw up all over it."

After a few days of doing nothing and running out of money fast, Liz gets a job with an escort service. This is even better than the massage parlor because she can stay at home with Tommy and study or watch television when she is not making money. She and Tommy like to watch daytime television best. That's when all the good reruns are on: *Andy of Mayberry*, *Happy Days*, and *Perry Mason*.

She likes working for the escort service. She likes to think of herself as a high-class call girl. She has a different clientele now. Her nails are done in Cadillac Red and she wears stockings and garter belts underneath her dresses, but otherwise she still looks like someone you would want to take home to meet your folks – as long as she wears her sleeves long.

She likes her customers. There is an American Indian named Sam who travels around the state and sells turquoise jewelry. He always gives her a ring or bracelet. He is a good lover and she sometimes runs her fingers through his long, thick black hair.

One time she is called to the Omni Hotel to be the date of a Japanese businessman. When she comes back to their apartment in South Miami, Tommy asks, "Was his dick small?"

"Yes," she answers.

"Was it smaller than mine?"

"Yes," she says.

She does not tell Tommy how gentle the man's hands were, how she floated in the bed as his fingers stroked her pale, punctured flesh like sheer silk scarves. She does not tell Tommy that if the Japanese man had not had a penis at all he still would be one of the best lovers she has ever taken money from – or not taken money from.

In her Comparative Religions class at school, they studied excerpts from *The Teachings of Buddha*. One story in particular has made a place for itself in her mind. In it a man has heard one of the gods singing. He climbs up a tree and when the god (who looks like a demon) comes by, he begs it to sing the song again. The god-demon agrees only if the man will leap to his death afterward. The song is so beautiful that the man agrees. After he hears the song, he lets himself fall from the tree as he agreed to do, but the god, now radiant and glorious, catches the man and sends him off to live a long and happy life. Liz feels as if she has been falling all her life, but she doubts there is anyone waiting to catching her.

She sits in the chair by her oval mirror in the bedroom. The bed is huge and takes up most of the floor space. She ties off her arm with the sash from her bathrobe and injects a needle of cocaine mixed with smack into her vein. Whenever she sticks a needle into her arm, she feels as if she is standing in the doorway between life and death. She cleans out the needle and sprays the mirror with bloody water. All junkies do this. There are tiny drops of blood along the top of the yellow wall where Tommy has created an artistic work of pointillism. She lies down on the bed, her tongue twisting in her mouth as everything around her turns darker and brighter at the same time.

Liz has often felt that if you could open her up from her breastbone down you would see an emptiness as wide as the universe inside. When she was little, Auntie's son would ride her on his shoulders all over the neighborhood. Her feet never had to touch the ground where the stickers and the bumblebees and the dog poop lay like traps for bare little feet. But then he went away to college and never came back for more than a day or two. She cannot remember when she finally realized that he was never coming back for good. The emptiness inside her seems to keep growing. Once it was just a tiny fissure but then the crack widened further and further, spreading like bad news in a small town.

Sometimes the tricks she goes on now are just drug parties with drug dealers and other hookers. They might be in an apartment in the north side of town, a bunch of people getting blasted on lines of cocaine and big chalky Quaaludes that hang in your throat. The world gets all frazzy, and Liz is not sure why this is pleasant. Actually, she doesn't even think about it any more than she thinks about why she has to eat or go to the bathroom. The drug dealers always give her something to take home to Tommy.

So far she has managed two semesters of junior college and gotten on the Dean's List both times. She is not sure why she bothers going to classes. She hasn't made any friends there, and it's not like she has a career plan, but Tommy is proud of her because she is a chick with some book smarts. And it is something to tell Auntie. In her Introduction to Psychology class, she learned that schizophrenics do not really have split personalities. Which is a good thing because it means that even if she does feel like two completely different people, she is not a schizophrenic.

The two people who she is – the hooker and the schoolgirl – sometimes get mixed up with each other. The whore writes her papers. The schoolgirl visits the men who call her. She likes imagining that they are in love with her. And then there is Tommy. She loves Tommy and the way he kisses her and never says anything mean to her. But she doesn't understand why it feels as if the world is a shattered plate glass window no matter who she is.

She thinks back to the massage parlor. One night there was a shy knock on the door. No one ever knocked. They just came in. She opened the door, and there was a man wearing a polka-dotted dress, black pumps and a black wig and looking exactly like her sixth grade teacher, Miss Washburn at North Columbus Elementary. "Do you give golden showers?" the man had asked. Liz had shaken her head, and said, "No, no, we don't." Thinking, well, of course, we do everything, but she could not bring herself to do that. What she felt for the man was a vast pity. But later when she told Tommy, they laughed about him – the freak who wanted someone to piss on him. Laughter is harder and harder to come by.

It is past midnight and she gets a call to go to the Newport Hotel in North Miami Beach. She goes and meets the guy. It is not a difficult trick, but not much fun either. The guy is a drug dealer. He gives her 150 bucks, but doesn't want to treat her like she's a person. That's OK. She's tired, and just needs to pay the rent. Besides, there is a leather jacket she wants to buy for Tommy. They have gotten on the methadone maintenance program so they do not have to spend money on heroin.

The high from the methadone is strong and satisfying, but they do not like having it doled out by a sour-looking nurse and having to pee in a cup every week or so to prove they are not still using smack. After they get their dose each morning, they eat breakfast by themselves at the IHOP.

On the way home, she is feeling more awake from the few lines of coke the guy miserly doled out, nothing even to take home for Tommy. She flies along the highway through downtown Miami. This is one of the things she loves – this highway at three in the morning. Curving down and then up and then: blast! the skyline spreading across the black cosmos. The sugar-sweet air swirling through the car windows. Her hair lifting from her neck in the wind, the road underneath smooth as pulled taffy. This must be how a dolphin feels, cruising along the ocean currents.

Tonight, however, there is a dog on I-95. Some kind of beagle, trotting along one of the six lanes of traffic. Liz is just coming into the three-layered cloverleaf grid and she pulls over, thinking she can get the dog into her car. Another car pulls behind her. The dog is between the two of them, looking at her and then back at the other car. A young man gets out of the other car. The two of them advance upon the dog from either direction. The dog looks again one way and then the next. Then he puts his forelegs on the concrete railing overlooking the highway below.

"Come here, boy," she says.

But the dog does not come to her. Instead, he leaps over the rail to the concrete far below. She stands there, the night solidifying like onyx around her. She wonders if she were someone else whether she could have coaxed the dog into her car. Then she is crying and the young man is holding her.

When she gets home, she does not wake Tommy. But as soon as it is morning, she calls Auntie. She cannot stop crying as she tries to tell Auntie about the dog. Life is so sad, she keeps thinking. Life is so sad. But while that refrain repeats itself in her head, another voice lies right underneath it like bone under the flesh. The other voice is saying, Life is so good, Life is so good. If she could just peel off the word sad, she could hear the other word. And she does hear it. She just doesn't know that she hears it. She's like someone in a coma. People are coming in, talking to her and holding her hand. She doesn't hear them, but their voices are keeping her alive until her eyes can flicker open.

It is not that much longer before she realizes that she can no longer turn tricks. Maybe it is only a week or so later that some kid calls her up and then when she gets to his house, he tries to rough it off her. She isn't frightened, just really angry. So angry that she reaches for Tommy's buck knife in her purse and scares the kid away from her.

"Just go away," he tells her. And she does.

The next day the nurse at the methadone clinic says that Tommy's urine has come back dirty. Tommy swears they're wrong, but Liz drives straight to her bank and finds their checking account wiped out. At home she slams a big book – *The Norton Anthology of English Literature Volume I* – into Tommy's chest and tells him to leave. He says he's sorry. He cries, but the next morning she takes him to the bus station. She buys him a ticket to Columbus. He stares at her, big brown eyes over high cheekbones. His lips are soft as he kisses her one last time.

"Go on," she tells him and then gets back in her car. She drives away, refusing to look into her rearview mirror.

The next day she doesn't go to the methadone clinic,

and she doesn't go to school for her final exams. Instead, she stays in her apartment, disconnects the phone and pulls down the shades. She does not turn on the television. She does not do anything but lie in her bed in a white slip, waiting.

She feels it circling the small yellow building of her apartment house. The hungry thing. Looking for a way to get in. But as in all those old horror movies, she knows the beast is already inside. Pain is perching above her like a vulture. They say that methadone withdrawal is worse than heroin. But that is not what scares her. What she braces herself for is the fall into that empty space of herself. The fall which has already begun. Maybe after all, something will catch her, something radiant and god-like that will cradle her like a newborn baby.

She waits to find out.

Singing in the Free World

I sang soprano in the prison choir. Each Sunday I sat in the front row, mid-section on the platform, facing the congregation. Between hymns I held my hands in my lap and watched the turtle-headed preacher in the pulpit beside us. The folds of fat in his neck jiggled as he railed against us. Every Sunday a couple of the older women would get filled with the Holy Ghost, raise their hands in the air and call out, "Oh, Lord. Yes, Jesus."

The first time I saw them do that, I remember catching Jesse's eye. She was standing over to the side waiting to do her solo, and her lips twitched slightly as if she was going to laugh, but then she resumed that dark mask.

Jesse was the choir leader. Thin and ageless, hard as the highway that hummed on the other side of the swamp past the fences, Jesse had a voice that seized our hearts, made us love life and let us ride the backs of notes that flew out of the stagnant prison air. Once I told her that she had the most beautiful voice I had ever heard, and she had smiled, her face turning into a heart.

"Thanks, professor," she said. Some of the inmates called me that because I worked in the prison library and had read just about every book in the place. And though I didn't let on much, I'd had a good private school education and had learned Latin and French up through the ninth grade anyway. Then my mother died of congenital heart failure, and six weeks later Daddy married a rattle snake disguised as a woman who thought that it was a waste of money to send me to that "ridiculous snobby" school. When I was sixteen, I took my father's car and drove away, ripping out the rearview mirror and tossing it on the road behind me.

A couple of months after I joined the choir, the preacher gave his famous "movie" sermon. I guess he did it about once a year because all the long-timers knew the lesson by heart and sometimes joked about the "dirty smut in your movie".

On that windy March Sunday, the preacher riveted his head toward each one of us like one of those wooden carnival fortune-tellers and told us that when we died, every single thought we'd ever had and every single thing we'd ever did would be projected on a movie screen for every single other person WHO HAD EVER LIVED to see. And even though I didn't believe him for a second, I started to feel uncomfortable, the seams in my dress began to itch against my skin and I had to wriggle my back around in the hard folding chair. I kept thinking about my grandfather who had been an Episcopalian priest and died when I was seven. I saw him sitting in a dark movie theater watching me with my genitals spread open like a split tomato for various men to use, their sweaty crumpled hundred dollar bills on the bed stand, or seeing me con his widow, my grandmother, out of fifty bucks so I could get a fix. And I started to feel as if I wanted to go into the bathroom and vomit.

That afternoon I sat on one of the vinyl couches in the big dayroom in the dorm and stared through a trickle of rain at the compound: the low, cinderblock dorms, the cafeteria, the factory, the administration building, the school and the chapel in the middle. Our own little village, gray in the slanting rain. I thought how different the place was from what I expected – which was Alcatraz or something. I had figured there would be guard towers and sharp-shooting ex-marines pointing rifles down at us. But all they had were a couple of high fences topped with razor wire surrounding a few hills, some bored women in uniforms running the dorms and a half a dozen male guards patrolling the grounds lazily. And yet, though it looked almost like a college campus, it might just as well have been Alcatraz or Raiford or Sing-Sing because once your freedom is gone, nothing else really matters.

As I sat there in the dayroom, listening to women squabble about who took whose soap or whatever they were missing, I begin to ache for the Free World. Just to see it and smell it. I'd been locked up almost a year and something had begun to freeze up inside me. I needed new sights. My eyes needed them in a physical sense. My only hope of going outside before my parole date, which wasn't for another fifteen months and twelve days, was through the choir. They'd gone on a trip to the outside the past Christmas. I had been inspired to join soon after. So even though I was sitting there, thinking I ought to quit the choir so I wouldn't have to listen to those whacked-out sermons, I knew I would not quit. Could not quit. Not now.

We had church on Sunday mornings and vespers on

Wednesday night. The choirmaster did not come to vespers, and so a 180-pound check forger, who may have had a few piano lessons in junior high school, played haltingly on the upright and we tried to follow. I sang softly because I was never sure of the beat or anything else. Jesse had to direct us. I would follow her lips and her icy glances over at the pianist. Even so, I preferred the Wednesday night services. They seemed somehow holier because there was no hellfire and damnation, just singing and praying. I especially enjoyed the walk back to the dorm afterward, sometimes stopping at the steps that led down to the building to look up at the milky way glittering like a cache of stolen diamonds, carelessly strewn across a lacquer table. I had the sense that none of this was real – that if I could just peel back the surface of things, I would be able to dog paddle across the dimensions to that place where reality really is. Then the officer of the night would open the door and say, "Inmate, you're fixing to get locked out." If that happened, even if I were banging on the door to get in, I would have been considered an escapee, and so I would hurry in because I didn't know how to peel back the surface and I had learned the hardest way to respect the laws of the earthly – especially the one about "Thou shalt not sell cocaine to undercover police officers."

One Sunday after the service a free woman from the prison ministry came up to me and said, "God has a plan for you. I looked at your face, and I saw it." Glowing with the gospel, she meant what she said. But I knew that she was fooled by my pale, almost blue skin and my long filmy hair. To everyone else I appeared to be a model prisoner, going to my job function in the keypunch training program everyday, attending classes and regular counseling. But at night I dreamt about bloody needles and warm guns and piles of cocaine around me like snow drifts. I didn't tell her that the only reason I even came to church was because I kept hoping the choir would get to go on a trip outside, even if I had to wait to Christmas.

But I did not have to wait for Christmas.

On Palm Sunday, the choirmaster told us that we would be leaving the compound on Easter. We were going to sing in a Free World church. Hallelujah!

On Good Friday I stood in the dinner line with my bent metal tray in my hands. It was chicken for the tenth night in a row. I put my tray out and took the chicken even though I would not eat it because I figured the sooner they got rid of it, the sooner we'd get a change in the menu. I headed over to the table where some of my junkie buddies from the dorm sat when I looked across the room and saw Jesse sitting where she almost always sat – alone. I changed course and went to her table.

"Hey, Jesse. Gonna sing anything special on Easter?" I asked after I sat down.

"Nope," she said. She ate a spoonful of creamed corn. I have hated creamed corn since kindergarten. About all that I could stand to eat were the crackers and peanut butter and jelly mixture that looked like a blob of shit but tasted all right.

"I'm not going to sing at all," she said after a while.

The peanut butter stuck in my throat.

"Why not?" I asked when I could talk again.

"I'm not going," she said and ate some more, chewing everything methodically.

"Don't you want to go?" I asked Jesse.

"I can't," she said. Her eyes were as black as the bottoms of the spoons I once used to cook heroin. She glared at me for an instant and then looked back down at her food. I didn't ask any more questions. I just ate the rest of my crackers and peanut butter and jelly and drank my milk to the rhythm of clattering metal trays and metallic conversations, the strange chorus of 640 women laughing, arguing and gossiping.

"Well, we'll miss you," I said as I got up to leave. She nodded and flicked her eyes up at me. There was something unreadable, unknowable in those eyes.

Easter morning we got up while it was still dark, dressed and then filed out across the compound. In our pink, blue or gold prison dresses, we resembled a bunch of Easter eggs. As we stepped through the double gates, I looked over at a Technicolor sunrise. Free World.

"It's a damn shame Jesse can't come," Delores said breaking the morning silence. Delores always stood next to me on the platform. I had known her before I came to prison when she used to sell good brown Mexican dope in Coconut Grove.

"Why can't she come?" I asked Delores.

"Girl, she's got so much time, she ain't gonna see the free world until she's as old as Moses. She murdered her own mama," Delores said as she climbed up the steps of a dingy white bus with wire mesh on the windows.

"What?" I asked, following her up the steps. I hadn't known Jesse's crime. Those things weren't discussed much in prison; our past was the only privacy we had.

"Her mama was nasty. She put Jesse's little sister on the streets of Liberty City when the girl was fourteen. Jesse got herself a pistol and shot her down like a dog," Delores said.

I was too stunned to say anything else. I sat down in an empty seat and stared out the window as the choirmaster closed the doors of the bus and drove off. I was thinking of my own mother and how much I missed her. I had never really let myself stop long enough to notice that the big hole in my life I had kept stuffed with drugs and men was where she had been. I had been lucky, I realized, to have had someone like that even if it was not for very long. And I felt sad and a little joyful at the same time. Sad for myself and for people like Jesse and joyful that I was outside of those fences and that I was seeing the world in the full glory of Easter morning.

The bus pulled into a parking lot in Ocala. We got out and stood before a steepled Baptist church. Beautifully dressed black people – bright as butterflies – streamed around us and through the wooden double doors. They smiled at us, and I'm sure I wasn't the only one who felt they were some kind of angels. Inside, the church-goers listened politely as we sang "Morning Has Broken," the only song we knew really well. Then we joined the congregation in the pews and the home choir took over, older women with chests that had room for God and all his host.

The preacher had a voice as rich as hot fudge. Every time he said the name "Jesus" he'd tap real fast with his feet. We could feel that little step building into something grand. We were burning with hot, breathing life. The preacher's words rang out over our heads and filled the building. Amen, we shouted. It got inside us. It swept up our breath and moved in the cavities of our hearts. The light cascaded through the windows onto our shining faces.

The preacher told us to rise and hold hands. My hand wrapped around that of a tall copper-skinned man, and I immediately sensed something between me and that handsome man. I was digging it bigtime, the feel of his cool palm against the slight dampness of mine, the gentle pressure of his fingers around my fingers. And then, all at once, something came flooding up from the soles of my feet and I felt a tremendous implosion, then an immediate flight like a flock of birds rising in my chest.

And in the next moment the sky that was growing inside me turned into ocean. And I knew that this feeling had nothing to do with the man or with being in the Free World. It was as if every molecule inside me was whispering with the voices of ten thousand souls saying, I am, I am, I am.

I went back to the compound, dizzily euphoric and yet unsure of what to do with this thing I'd been given as if someone had handed a baby to me and told me to take care of it. I did not know who I could tell about that feeling, who would understand. I walked around the compound like someone in a waking dream. I could still smell the copper-skinned man's cologne on my fingers.

That evening during free hour I sat out on the bleachers by the softball field watching some of the women practice. After a while I realized someone had sat near me. It was Jesse, humming to herself like a river.

"Jesse," I said. She looked over at me.

"Hi, professor. How was the trip outside?" she asked.

I edged closer to her.

"It was strange, Jesse," I said. "Really strange. I felt God."

"You?" she asked. "Tell me what it felt like."

"It felt like cocaine and heroin mixed together, but better," I said. "And it didn't make my teeth grind."

She laughed.

"No," I said, "Not really like that. It was like if you're standing somewhere and a sinkhole opens up underneath you. You know how the water runs in those underground rivers. It's always there but you never know it until the ground drops and you fall in."

"Yeah, Frankie," she said. "I think I know what you mean."

"You do?" I asked.

"I feel it every time I sing. I know something is keeping

me alive in here. I know it isn't me, girl," she said. I looked at the sharp bones of her face like cut crystal, the deep gloss of her black skin and the way she had her hands folded together with two fingers pointing outward.

It took three days for the feeling to wear off. Then there was a fight in the dorm between two of the younger women, girls actually, emotional as fifth graders. The two of them loved the same person, another prison romance gone awry. They screamed at each other suddenly in the middle of the dorm between bunks. Anger and fear spat through us all like lightning leaping from one conduit to another. One girl took a ceramic cup and creamed the other one across the skull. Then we all got quiet as blood seeped through the blond tangled hair. The uniforms came in and took her to the hospital. The other went straight to lock up, and no one in the dorm said much else that night.

Lights went out at ten, and I lay in the darkness. One by one the breathing of the women slowed down to a single chord. I ran my fingers along the cinderblock wall behind my bed. For three days I had been free. Now, I was back. Thick wire mesh covered the windows. The walls were cold and hard. I had come back to what I'd always known, even before I was locked up – prison. I felt as though I was falling back asleep into a dream, the same dream I had every night. But this time there was something different, a voice like a thread of smoke that softly brushes your cheek. It was Jesse's voice, singing, and I had the feeling that it would always be there – even when all I could hear was a silence as vast as the universe.

The Hawk's Shadow

I had never been happier: the smell of Noxema, my pink skin still simmering, and the ocean exploding into white feathers outside as we lay in the twin beds that first night. The sliding glass door of Laura's bedroom stood open so that we could hear the waves murmuring like the heartbeat of the world. Salty breezes licked our cheeks.

"Are you asleep?" I asked.

Silence. I waited for a moment. Then she pursed her lips and made a farting sound. We giggled madly.

Laura Taylor was my best friend. Lanky and blond and terrible, Laura, even at eleven, made her older brothers' friends grin nervously and lose their composure; the billiard balls went berzerk when she loped into the den. She had two brothers. Jonathan, the first born, looked like a Kennedy, and the other like a killer. His name (the killer's) was Carl, but everyone called him Stub.

On the second day, Laura and I were waxing the old surfboard that Jonathan never used anymore, when

Jonathan, Carl and three of their friends came out on the deck. The brothers ignored us, but their buddies, all around sixteen or so, kept glancing over at Laura, her strong tan arms and her body just budding into her bikini.

"That's not a surfboard. It's the *Queen Mary*," one of them laughed. "You're never gonna get that ship to sea."

Laura tossed the wax at him, and he laughed some more. I sat back on the deck and felt the sand gritting into my bare thighs. They were all laughing and joking. Soon someone started talking about girls, and then they began teasing Stub for doing something unspecified with a large homely girl from school. Talking about her, one of them said, "Anyone seen any beached whales around here?"

And like a fool, I opened my big mouth and said, "Just Stub." I had meant it good naturedly, but as soon as the words were out I realized their meanness. Even though Stub had always frightened me a little, I felt sorry for him. Laura was her father's favorite, and Jonathan his mother's. Fat, lumbering Stub was nobody's favorite.

He moved faster than I would have thought him capable and stood over me. "Shut up, nigger lips," he sneered.

I looked quickly over at Laura, but she just laughed. And I shut up, tucking in my lips, which had been split open in a bike accident the previous Christmas.

I was staying with Laura's family at their beach house for a couple of weeks that summer. My mother had told me never to go past my ankles in the water because of undertows. But each day we swam out past the breaking waves and dolphined through the surf. Around noon sometimes we strolled down the mile or so of sand to the Beach Club and ordered hamburgers and cokes with lemon slices that we never had to pay for. Laura just signed the bill. Later we might go into the locker room and smoke Winstons.

"Watch me, Holly," Laura said one day when we were bored. She opened her mouth, her lips pressed tightly against her teeth, and blew perfect smoke rings into the air. The room smelled like wet concrete the way locker rooms do, and we liked that smell; it seemed adult. I couldn't blow smoke rings, but I could make the smoke come fuming from my nose and cross my eyes at the same time. The sight sent Laura into hysterics.

We were naked, except for the towels wrapped around our bodies. Laura lifted her leg and farted, which was another thing I could not do on command. Maybe it was the way I was raised. An only child, no older brothers to clue me in on the real mysteries of life. And yet outside the locker room, Laura could metamorphose into someone else entirely, inscrutable and beautiful as a magazine photo. I couldn't pull that poise over me the way she did. I was the clown, bumping my big lips into windows.

Laura and I usually fended for ourselves as far as our meals went, but one night we went with her brothers and her mother to the Club for dinner. Laura's father was still in town on business, and I was disappointed that he wasn't coming to dinner with us. He was the only member of the family besides Laura who ever acknowledged my existence.

We sat at the round table, bedecked with white tablecloth, several plates for each setting and a slew of knives and forks and spoons. Laura's mother and the older son carried on a hungry flirtation with each other, while Carl sullenly glowered at the rest of the diners and Laura and I suppressed our prepubescent giggling. But the whole family joined in to laugh heartily at my sudden shock when a tall silent waiter hovered over my salad holding a huge wooden cylinder in his hand like a club. I looked questioningly at Laura, who said, "He wants to know if you want pepper on your salad."

I nodded at the waiter, and he sharply twisted the pepper mill, sending a little shower of black pellets onto my salad. The fresh pepper carried an odor of worldliness; I relished it, allowed it to imprint on my senses. Laura's mother and Jonathan rolled their eyes at each other that Laura should have such a piteous rube for a friend, but I knew that she treasured me.

I was the one who had explained our sixth grade math problems to her, I had written a poem for her when she needed one for class, and one time at the park where we all played tetherball and basketball, I had pushed Christopher Jenkins off his bicycle when he said she couldn't play with us because she was rich. "She is not," I had said indignantly even though I knew her father ran the largest life insurance company in town. But most importantly, no one else could make her laugh the way I did. We spoke a separate language, a silly one with made-up words and private jokes. It was the core of our childhood.

The two weeks passed, and we still hadn't learned how to surf. But we had developed other interests. Every Saturday night, the teenagers took command of the Club. We wanted to go, and we spent the whole day perfecting our tans, practicing new dance steps, and giggling and wondering if anyone would glance our way.

When Laura's brothers piled into Jonathan's baby blue Mustang, we ran outside to catch a ride, but Carl slammed the door and told us we should go drown ourselves. Jonathan just grinned and hit the accelerator, spitting tiny pebbles at us from the driveway. Laura's mother, wearing blue puff slippers, took us. Her long nails tapped the steering wheel, and she didn't say a word when we got out in front of the Club.

Lanterns hung around the patio, and mid-sixties music, not the stuff of revolutions, but Beach Boys and Blood

Sweat and Tears, swam over our heads as we loitered moon-poisoned along the sides, glancing at the older boys and girls, men and women to us, as they danced in slow, circular clutches. Jonathan danced with a beautiful long-haired girl most of the night, and Carl stood on the side, watching.

Laura and I found a spot where we could look out at the water and still hear the music. One song, in particular, pierced right through me, a deep bluesy voice and a saxophone solo, spreading like a burst blood vessel. We held our breaths in dark suspense, imagining the way it must feel, those arms wrapped about you, that mouth brushing your neck and your hair, those hips pressing against yours. What happens when someone is that close to you, I wondered. Do you evaporate? I could think of nothing else.

The next day when it was time for me to go home, Laura had to go to a tennis lesson with her mother, and we waved carelessly to each other as she rode off in the big new Fleetwood. I stayed at the beach house to wait for my own mother to pick me up in her six-year-old Pontiac.

The house was L-shaped with the den in the bottom part of the L. I could hear Jonathan's laughter as he and his friends played pool. I wanted to avoid him because his cold good looks frightened me almost as much as Carl's small black eyes. I walked down the long hallway past the boys' room and into Laura's bedroom just waiting for the honk of my mother's car horn, and wishing Laura hadn't gone. From the sliding glass door, I could see the afternoon storm clouds marshalling above the ocean. The storms came rolling in at nearly the same exact moment every day. That was usually when Laura and I would come in and eat Fritos and drink cokes and maybe watch television or just talk. I wondered if she would miss me.

I crossed the cool tile floor, touched the headboard where I had scratched my name. Then I heard a noise and looked up. Carl stood in the bathroom between Laura's bedroom and his.

"Holly, come here," he said. He had never called me by my name before, and his voice was soft as cotton. He wore only a pair of white underwear. I stared at him. Folds of white belly hung over his briefs; his face was screwed up in that permanent scowl. "Come here," he said. I obediently but very slowly walked to the bathroom. In school that year I had learned that baby chickens will run for cover at the sight of a hawk's shadow, but they will ignore the shadow of a duck or a stork. This happens as soon as they step out of their shells because they are born with the fear of hawks' shadows. The fear I felt as I stood in the bathroom, Carl's heavy breath on my neck, seemed to come from a very old place inside me.

He had the medicine chest open and pointed to a cigarette there on the shelf.

"Is that Laura's cigarette?" he asked. I shook my head.

"Does Laura smoke?" he asked. I wondered why he was asking. Did he really care?

"No," I said, lying instinctively. "I mean, I don't think so."

He had taken my arm; his hand felt oily and warm and then he sat down on the lid of the toilet seat and pulled me onto his knee. The confusion of the moment swallowed me. I knew that he had never liked me. Did he suddenly want me for a girlfriend, I wondered, the terror building in my chest. I gulped down the fear, thinking, hoping that Laura's other brother would come in on us.

But then he said, "If you make any noise, I'll break your neck." His right hand slid up my back. And then his other hand rose from my leg and came toward the small mound of my breast. I watched the space between his hand and my striped shirt narrow. In an instant I felt his hand on me, squeezing me. My scream echoed off the green tiled walls. He threw me out of the bathroom, and I flew like a wind-tossed gull. Then a second later, I hit the hard floor by Laura's bed. The sky exploded, and Carl stood above me. I looked over at the closed bathroom door. Carl's hand covered my mouth as he sank on top of me.

Rain ran along my face as I waited outside for my mother. Wet tar smell, tires whistling on slick pavement. Cars kept speeding past, and rain dripped from the tip of my nose, from my chin, from my eyelashes into a wide ocean at my feet.

I thought about the upcoming year when Laura and her brothers and I would all be going to the same school. I thought about her house and the new whirlpool bathtub she'd gotten, and I remembered the Barbie doll collection that we dressed up when we were younger, giving them parties to go to and the kind of lives we knew we would some day lead. I thought about all the nights we spent at each other's house, laughing in one of our canopy beds until our tired bodies could laugh no longer. I thought about the secrets we had shared, the coded looks that linked us like lovers' hands. But nothing could remove the feel of the blood now dried on my legs or the thudding pain inside me.

The cars kept passing as I stood there among the sandspurs and the raindrops, alone.

Fire and Light

My mother struck a match from the glossy white matchbook she had picked up at the rehearsal dinner two nights earlier. The small yellow flame stood straight as a steeple as she brought it to the end of a Winston she had begged from the best man.

"Thirty minutes late," she hissed, eradicating the flame with a sharp snap of her hand. "I don't know why I let you do this." Her cobalt eyes passed across me in my long white gown with the scalloped lace neck. I stared in the mirror as I pinned the mantilla in my dark hair. I had chosen not to wear a veil, and I looked as if I were entering a convent instead of getting married.

"I don't know why either," I said. Her gaze locked into mine like a deadbolt fitting into place. I hadn't seen her smoke a cigarette in five years. And hadn't seen her upset since I don't know when. She didn't even really get mad when Sneak pawned her typewriter and then swore up and down he didn't do it. She calmly told him if it didn't appear on her desk by the next day, she would have a little chat with his probation office. Not surprisingly, the typewriter returned. Sneak said he had found the culprits and convinced them to return it.

I turned from her and stared out the window of the choir dressing room into the small concrete foyer outside where I had watched teenagers making out when I was a small girl. I would hide from their view in this very same room. My mother, an avowed agnostic, had been the church administrator since I was a baby, and I knew every secret hidden in every stone of this building. I used to scale the walls, clinging onto the yellow granite blocks, and once I crawled through the ventilation system.

"One week out of high school," my mother muttered. "I had better plans for you."

It was true, just a week earlier the Class of '72 had received their tassels to hang from their rearview mirrors. That seemed all there was to show for the whole twelve-year ordeal. I had graduated third in my class, but did not go to graduation, was busy riding the streets and drinking tall boys with Sneak in my yellow Volkswagen instead. I didn't know how to tell my mother that I hadn't meant any of this – this getting married – that it was only because my ego was injured when he'd slept with my best friend and he was begging me to forgive him and I was mad at her, my mother, for some reason I couldn't even remember. I had said, yes, sure, and hoped like hell that something would come along and get me out of it. Then the invitations were sent out, and the Episcopal church where I had spent all my childhood days was dressed in flowers and someone unrolled a long white runner down the aisle, the apostles and Jesus looking on morosely from glass panes of blue, green, yellow and red.

I looked down the concrete hallway to the gymnasium where I had played basketball with the janitor in the summers while my mother kept watch over the holy coffers. The janitor was my best friend. I was seven years old, fatherless, and lived for the fa-toomp, fa-toomp, fa-toomp of the basketball, the rubbery feel of it against my hand and my hair swishing madly around my face and into my mouth as I whirled around the glossy floor and then flung the ball as hard as I could toward the basket, which I almost always missed. Some kids from the neighborhood called me a "nigger lover" and said my mother was a Yankee and that she had unfairly won the war. I never believed I was a Yankee. My poor mother from Amherst might still "pawk the caw" but my life was the worship of bare feet, rain puddles, sandspurs, palmettos, giant multicolored grasshoppers and alarmingly pink azaleas that smothered the city in spring.

Someone knocked on the door. Sneak had finally shown up, high as the stratosphere, but that was to be expected, I suppose, since Sneak had begun to acquire a substantial heroin habit. My mother leaned over and kissed me dryly. I wasn't sure if she was more depressed about my impending marriage or the fact that Sneak's mother was wearing a dress the same aqua color as she wore.

The church where we were married was not an ordinary church. It was established in 1870, just about the time my mother unfairly won the war. At first they built one of those little clapboard chapels which they moved around the area of Riverside until they finally landed on the spot where it is now, and a new bigger church was built. But in the spring of 1901, a terrible fire ignited in a cigar factory in Jacksonville – a hot, blazing, church-burning fire. The new sanctuary crumbled to ashes and rubble, but the little wooden chapel by the Grace of God survived the flames, and the Sunday after the great Jacksonville fire, the congregation gathered together in the humble chapel and started over. By 1920 the church had a new big chapel built of dark red brick with an Olympic-sized swimming pool and a gymnasium. Later another, more elaborate and ornate sanctuary was built with Tudor arches and carved stone. This was where I stood next to my heavy-lidded groom and swore to love him in sickness and health until death do us part. Prison parted us long before death.

I hadn't even gotten used to the marriage before it was over. But I had the feeling that it wasn't much like other marriages. We hardly ever made love. Sneak would say he was going out for a pack of cigarettes and come back five, six hours later, stoned and burning holes in his shirts as he nodded off, cigarette dangling from his fingers, unable to remember my name. Then one day he didn't come back at all. He'd gotten busted with a back seat full of someone else's stereo speakers.

I sat with Sneak's mother in the courtroom. She didn't like me much, and made me feel as if this was all somehow my fault.

"Ten years," the judge said with a bang of his gavel that resonated through my bones. Ten years for a lousy burglary charge? Sneak turned around and looked helplessly at the two of us, his mouth open, pale eyes stricken. My heart crumpled, and his mother clutched my hand, which surprised me, but I figured she had to hold onto something. I was going to miss Sneak's high cackling laugh that shook him so hard he seemed as if he would float away, but I would not miss him as much as his mother would. He was devoted to her. My mother had said that was his only good quality and that you could tell how a man would treat his wife by the way he treated his mother.

After that it was like being a widow. I worked at the Southern Life Insurance Company with my mother-in-law. Southern Life was a giant of an insurance company in a town that thrived on insurance companies. Because of the early fire and the yellow fever epidemic before it, life seemed more precarious in Jacksonville and life insurance something they all believed in.

I worked in the mailroom and played nickel poker on my lunch hours with my co-workers. My mother-in-law worked on the seventh floor. I never had to see her during work hours unless I bumped into her in the cafeteria while I was picking up a sausage biscuit with mustard during my morning break.

My boss was a lady who had that dyed-black hair look that went to the beauty parlor every week and wore lipstick so red and dark it looked as if she drank blood instead of cup after cup of coffee. I had never met such an unabashed hypocrite in my entire life. I was awed and amazed when she'd pick up the phone with a scowl, knowing it was someone she despised – and she despised everyone – and then break into a smile as pretty as sunrise and say in a melodic voice, "Hello, honey."

Toward the end of August, my mother-in-law got ill and had to take a leave of absence – it was embarrassment over Sneak as much as anything else. But her illness was a boon for me because I got her parking space in the pay lot right across from the building. I would not be late anymore, not be scowled at by those sangria lips as I hurried in, having had to park five or six blocks away and run through the early morning heat to get to the yellow and turquoise square box that was the Southern Life Building. Oh, happy day, as I pulled into that parking lot in my little yellow Volkswagen Beetle and was shown into parking space number 35 between a Lincoln Continental and a Cadillac De Ville by an old guy with a cigar butt wedged between his gray lips.

The old guy had a helper, a young black man who often parked the cars for the patrons. Soon as I stepped out of my car, the helper smiled at me – a real smile, not like the Dragon Lady of the mailroom's smile.

"Don't you work too hard now," he said to me with a grin, and I couldn't help grinning right back.

Every day was like that, except we started talking more and more. His name was Willie and I told him about Sneak being in prison, which nobody at the company was supposed to know, but they all did. Sometimes after just a couple of weeks you can feel like you've known someone since you were in diapers. At the end of the day I would linger and tell Willie about the mailroom, how I hated it, how my feet hurt in the stupid pumps I had to wear. If the old guy was not around, we would share a reefer and gaze up at the late afternoon sky so far, far above as the sunlight slowly drained from the wide blue basin, washing against the bottoms of the soft purple clouds.

None of the buildings around us were very old. Downtown Jacksonville had been obliterated in the inferno of 1901. The fire began at 12:30 in the afternoon and within hours it had become a conflagration. The flames had rushed to the banks of the river like a flock of yellow birds coming in for a landing. By ten p.m. that night all that was left of downtown was the shell of the old courthouse, the Astor Building (made out of iron) and the monument to the confederate soldiers, who had lost the war so unfairly to my mother.

Willie kept saying I ought to come have lunch with him someday. At first I put him off.

"I only get an hour, Willie," I said, leaning against the fender of my car.

"You think I'm getting sweet on you. It ain't that. I wouldn't do that to a man who's doing time, try to take his old lady from him," he said, mouth pinched serious and eyebrows close together, stocky compact body like a boxer. "But I know you'd like that food down there. Girl, you ain't had soul food till you've been to the Ashley Street Cafe."

Down on that part of Ashley Street, you never saw a white face. But Sneak used to go there all the time. He had been to the Ashley Street Cafe and said it was "the tits". Sneak wasn't afraid of what anyone thought. He reminded me of my mother in that way.

"You scared to go?" Willie asked.

I shook my head. I wasn't. And I did want some soul food, as long as it was just friendship with Willie. To tell the truth, he felt like the best friend I'd had in a while. There was no one in the mailroom I could talk to.

So one day after sorting mail all morning long, something I showed a natural-born talent for, I stepped out of the frosty air-conditioned yellow and turquoise box and saw Willie watching for me across the street. Big Jim, the city whistle, blew out twelve noon in a deep bellow. Funny how you could hear it all over town.

Just seeing Willie made me smile. He crossed over and we started walking toward Ashley Street and the best soul food in town, not minding the tail-end-of-summer heat. I never did mind it, the way it swallows you and won't let you out until you've just about suffocated. Then it's gone, and autumn makes you want to cry.

The kind of soul food I love is cornbread, collard greens and beef stew. In the crowded, sizzling cafe, we sat at a banged-up linoleum counter and studied the menu items painted up on the wall above the stoves, where big pots of food waited, steaming and flavorful. Two ladies, one fat with jiggly arms and one skinny, dished up the meals onto thick white plates. They didn't even look at me funny. I sopped my cornbread in the stew gravy, and ate potatoes, carrots and thick chunks of simmering beef. The greens had that sharp vinegary taste that tingles the very tip of your tongue.

"You like this, Margaret?" Willie asked.

I nodded and kept eating.

"You sure you like this food? You don't have to eat it if you don't like it," he said, laughing. "Damn, I never saw a girl eat like you do. And you so skinny, too."

Then I laughed. His friends teased him about me, and he said, "Aw, leave me alone. She's somebody's lady. We're friends." He smiled down at his neck bones and rice. I nudged him and we both laughed and smirked like a couple of kids who know something that nobody else knows. What we knew was that we could be friends – white and black, man and woman – and that's all there was to it.

The next morning when I pulled my yellow Volkswagen beetle into the pay lot across the street from the yellow and turquoise box, I did not see Willie. I did see a shiny Chrysler in parking space number 35.

"You cain't park here no more," the old guy who owned the lot said to me. "We don't allow that here."

"Allow what?" I asked.

"White people don't mix with niggers in my lot," he said.

"Goddamn," I said and just sat there for a moment, my hand on the stick shift.

"Go on," he said. "Get outta here. Willie ain't around here no more either."

I couldn't even hate him; it would have been like hating a brick. Because I figured he was that stupid.

I was late, but I didn't care. I had lost my mother-in-law's parking space and that meant trouble. And I was lonely. So I started getting drunk with my co-workers after work and I slept with one of the guys – a nice, peach-skinned fellow; no one seemed to mind. Then I started stealing money from the company which is why they tell people never to send cash. If they sent cash to pay their bills, the envelope went straight into my pocket. The Dragon Lady would send me smoldering looks when she thought I wasn't looking, but she didn't know I was stealing. She couldn't imagine anyone ever being more hypocritical than herself. It would have hurt her pride. We just smiled and smiled at each other. Sometimes I could see the fillings on her back molars.

I didn't like stealing the money, but my fingers were unable to resist when I felt that extra weight to the envelope. One day after work, I sat in my car, and pulled the envelopes out from under my skirt where I had tucked them into my underpants since I didn't have pockets that day. I opened the envelopes and counted the grimy dollar bills. What was the point, I wondered, leaning my head against the leather-covered steering wheel. I cursed Sneak for being so stupid and getting sent to prison, leaving me here in this town all alone, this town that felt like ten coats of varnish. Then I knew something. I needed to find Willie. He could use this money. At least I still had a job.

My car crawled along Ashley Street. I stared at the faces, some smiling, some scowling. No one looked familiar. I drove around blocks, cruising slowly wherever I saw a group of people, but I realized I didn't really know where he hung out, who his other friends were. All I had known was a smiling face. I drove in circles, getting dizzy from the heat and carbon monoxide. Finally, I parked in front of the Ashley Street Cafe, got out of my car and peered inside. It was closed, empty, gloomy, haunted-feeling. People walking by looked at me in my little work outfit and pumps from the corners of their eyes. My shoulders slumped down, my hair hung around my elbows. I threw the dollar bills like so much old tissue into the gutter, wiping the tears from my face with my sleeve. A group of slick dudes watched me, laughed and said, "That bitch has lost her mind."

I got back in my yellow Volkswagen and swore I'd never go back to work at Southern Life again.

I moved out of the garage apartment where Sneak and I had lived for six whole weeks and back in with my mom. I hung around the swimming pool at her apartment complex where I ran into guys from the navy with oily accents who wanted to flirt and have sex, but I could never get past those accents. So I flashed my diamond at them and said my husband was coming back from out of town any day now.

My mom and I sometimes went out for dinner to a little Italian place with the requisite red-checked table-cloths and candles in old Chianti bottles. Jacksonville had once been called Cowford and was founded by a thirty-year-old man named Isaiah Hart, she told me once as we rode across the sleek new bridge arching over the St John's that was named after him. When you drove over that bridge you could smell coffee from the Maxwell House plant and see the most painfully beautiful sunsets, sunsets that reminded me of the Bach cantatas I heard at church.

"How come you never went back north after Daddy died?" I asked one night, picking absently at the wax on the Chianti bottle. Yellow fingers of candle light stroked her face. I had never asked that question before, never wondered until now. I couldn't even remember my father. Now it seemed like a sin that she had kept me here.

"I don't know. I had a job, and being a woman, it wasn't so easy to get a decent job back then. I was trapped here by money just like you got trapped by that marriage," she said and sent me a look full of broken glass. She wore a gold medallion like a shield over her heart.

"I'm not trapped," I answered.

"The hell you aren't," she said.

I stared across the table at her, the wavy dark hair that fell to her shoulders, the high forehead and long thin nose.

Hot wax dripped on my hand, and I yanked it away.

One day I went over to the church to see my mother, for gas money or something. She'd gone off on an errand, so I wandered around the church, through the hallways and up the stairs into the library – a room with oriental rugs, thick red velvet curtains and a ceiling two stories high. No wonder people thought I acted rich. I had grown up in a castle.

I wandered into the next building. In the gymnasium I heard a fa-toomp, fa-toomp, fa-toomp. I looked in. There was a man, skin dark brown-red and hair a light brown-red. I knew him. His name was Lucius, and he had been one of Sneak's crowd in high school before Sneak became a junkie. He shot at the basket, missed and then saw me. We stared at each other for a long time.

"You the new janitor?" I asked.

He nodded. I came in and we shot hoops all afternoon.

I had never made love to a black man before Lucius. We treated each other like virgins and were as tender as two doves. I stayed with him in his upstairs apartment that the church provided in an old house just across the street. I parked my car several blocks away, so my mother would not know where I was. I did not want anyone to know where I was. I was in hiding. From the world. I had no cash so I had to pawn my ring. I didn't need much money. Lucius usually fed me breakfast – hotcakes, sausage, paint-thick coffee – and we had Fritos, onion dip and Schlitz malt liquor for dinner. At night we danced in his apartment. He taught me the fox trot and the Charleston. I imagined we looked like a couple in an old black and white movie, hands clasped, twirling around each other like the stripes on a candy cane.

From Lucius's bedroom window, I could see my mother arriving to work in the mornings. But I stayed locked away in the apartment, watching soap operas. I knew I was supposed to do something with my life. I was eighteen and a high school graduate. I was supposed to work or go to college or have babies or something, but I didn't know what. I was a married woman without a husband. Mainly I spent my time missing my childhood and wishing I could re-enlist.

Lucius wasn't much of a talker except late at night as we lay in bed with the light of a streetlamp casting a bluish hue across our skins. Then he would remark on my ears or my fingertips or the way my nose turned up at the end. "You got skin soft as rose petals, babycakes," he told me. "Soft as rose petals." His voice – smooth and rich as melted ice cream – gave me goosebumps.

"You know," I told him one night, "one time my girlfriend and I took some acid. We were only fifteen, I guess. And we were outside this strip shopping mall. Anyway, we set fire to a bubble gum wrapper. Then we dropped it and before you know it, the whole side of this creek is up in flames. We freaked out. The weird thing is that nobody else seemed to notice we had set this brush fire. No one called the fire department or anything. The fire just finally burned itself out."

Lucius was silent for a minute. Then he said, "You shouldn't be taking drugs, babycakes. Look what happened to your old man."

"Yeah, I know," I said. "We were just bored."

The next day my mother did not show up for work. She didn't go a second day either. Finally, I got dressed and went over to her office.

"Margaret," the receptionist said, wetting her old

cracker-dry lips. "Your mother tried to find you everywhere."

"I was out of town with some friends," I said.

"She had an emergency business meeting at the Diocese main office. Some money was embezzled from the bishop's account, and your mother is the only one smart enough to straighten it all out," the gray-haired woman said, twirling a pencil up in the air. "I think they want her to come work for the bishop."

I didn't say anything.

"She left something for you," she added and handed me an envelope. I walked outside and opened it. Divorce papers and a note saying that all I had to do was sign. My marriage certificate was also in the envelope. I guess she was giving me some sort of choice. The church hovered at my back.

I went back through the office building and through the alcove where the teenagers used to make out. I opened the heavy wooden side door to the Sanctuary. It was so quiet, the deep smell of old stones and velvet kneeling pads as familiar as the smell of my own skin. I still had the papers in my hand as I wandered up and down the pews in the soft-colored light. I had played so many lonely days in this cavernous sanctuary, pretending to be a princess or a pirate while the organist practiced next Sunday's anthem.

I walked up the steps that led to the altar area and into the enclosed section where altar boys and priests usually went about their business delivering communion. There was a water spigot for holy water, and a silver chalice and tall pillars of white wax in wooden candle holders that were carved in the image of angels. I saw some matches by one of the candles.

I took the matches and knelt before the altar. It was draped in a heavy white linen cloth. Jesus Christ towered above me, hands outstretched in the resurrection pose, bright red pieces of glass in his palms. I struck a match and lit the marriage certificate. It flamed brilliantly, paper crackling and shriveling into blackness. The fire reached up, smoked and then consumed itself. I went to the little spigot and poured water into the chalice. I anointed the last of the embers. Then I heard a noise and turned around.

"What the hell you doing, babycakes?" Lucius asked, hands on hips, big amber eyes studying me.

"I'm getting unmarried," I answered.

He snorted and then said, "Let me get you something to clean up that mess."

When he came back with the broom and dustpan, I told him I couldn't stay in Jacksonville any longer.

"Why not?" he asked. I noticed sweat trickling across the pores of his beautiful red-toned skin.

"I don't mean with you," I said, sweeping up the last curls of wet charred papers into the pan. "I can't stay in this town. This place where everything is north or south, black or white, this or that. I'm sick of the smell of the paper mill and seeing the used rubbers floating in the river. I want to try something new. I want to do something all on my own."

We walked outside. The smell of Indian summer hung in the oak trees, musty like the Spanish moss, dry like the palm fronds, and laced with an exquisite sort of pain.

I gazed at Lucius, the soft lips, thick curl of lash.

"You want to come with me?" I asked.

"No, baby," he said, "I got a good yoke here. I can't leave. This is my home. Besides, if I went you wouldn't really be doing it on your own."

I nodded and stared down at my feet, at the pink-painted toenails, the leather sandal straps, the blue veins and the bone ridges and pale skin.

"Bye, Lucius," I said. He leaned over and kissed my cheek. I thought about Willie and hoped like hell Lucius wouldn't get fired from the church for that kiss.

Later that day after I sold or pawned all my wedding presents, I left a note for my mother on her office desk, telling her I had gone to seek my fortune. I told her I would write when I had an address. I signed the divorce papers and left them there, too. Unfairly or not, my mother had won another war. Then I got in my car and drove off. I pulled onto the interstate and headed west.

During the great fire of 1901, smoke could be seen as far away as Raleigh, North Carolina. I wasn't looking back so all I could see was the blue sky, the yellow light of the sun, and the long gray road like a river of mercury before me.

Inside Out

On the day of my fourth wedding anniversary, I went to the mall, bought a set of drinking glasses on sale and then stopped at Mrs Fields for a macadamia nut white-chocolate chip cookie – a solitary celebration of sorts. Bobby was in Louisiana, jumping out of airplanes and running through swamps. He had been talking about getting out of the Navy one of these days, quitting the Seals. He was ready for some kind of change, but he didn't know what. I was feeling ready for a change, too.

I felt a tap on my shoulder, and in an instant I was fourteen years old again with three pairs of stolen panties in my pocket. Guilt started lighting up the consoles inside my head. I fought down the momentary panic, turned around and there was Alvin.

"Barbie, I thought that was you," he said.

"Alvin," I said. I swooped back into the warm waters of Lake Alice, college days, stoned, skinny-dipping with

Rip and Alvin and the rest of our crowd, brains cells hardening into petrified memories.

"Well, I don't see much of you these days," I said.

He shrugged. Work. Kids. That kind of thing.

"Don't you have any kids yet, Barb?" he asked.

"God, no, Alvin," I said. I still hadn't come up with the stock answer for this question. And how many zillion times had I been asked?

Alvin pulled out pictures.

"Kids are great," he said, "but a lot of work. A whole lot."

I feigned interest in the pictures. A boy and a girl in separate photos with dazed, almost shocked looks on their faces.

"Cute, Alvin," I said. "Very cute."

Our eyes met, and his were sympathetic as if he was thinking maybe it was just as well for me not to breed. Even at thirty-two, I wasn't exactly the mother type. My worst fear was that if I had a kid it would turn out like me.

"Hey, Rip is in town," he said after I handed back the pictures. "He's got some big client he's meeting here. I ran into him when he was getting some permits for a shoot."

"Really?" I said. A miniature seismic wave traveled up my spine. The girl behind the counter handed me my cookie, and I collected myself. "Oh, that's right. I heard he was supposed to be in town. I haven't checked my voice mail in days."

I wanted to find Rip and throttle him for not calling me. He was married now, but you don't have what we had for all those years and then just not call the person when you come in town. Marriage doesn't change something like that. At least it didn't for me. I mean, the sex part maybe but nothing else. Alvin's conversation sprang back to his kids like a rubberband.

I wrenched myself free from his scintillating discussion of chicken pox vaccines and strep throat and decided to leave the mall. It was hot outside even though it was only April, and the teenagers were just starting to slouch in like an army of slugs. I got into my car, fastened the seat belt and tried to marshal my emotions. It was then that I remembered dreaming about Rip not long ago. We were naked and rubbing together like fish in a shower somewhere and the water streaming over us was hot and then cold and then hot again. My dreams are not known for subtlety.

So he was here – on business, of course. Why hadn't he called me? Was his wife with him? Did she care? I mean, why would he tell her anything about me other than the fact that we were friends? I drove back toward the beach where Bobby and I were living in a house off the base. Funny thing about Bobby was that ever since we got married, he had total faith in me. I was the one who kept expecting me to screw up.

The day before our wedding, we had to go to a counselor because my rib was cracked and I was ready to call off the wedding, but my mother wouldn't let me do it without going to this counselor first. Mom had married two alcoholics. Bobby was a Navy Seal. He hardly ever drank. He was stable and even good for me, she said, and she wasn't going to let me throw this one away.

We were in the counselor's office. I was sitting next to Bobby and he was doing this fakey relaxed thing. He smiled at the counselor, a guy around fifty who looked like the therapist in *Ordinary People*, same helpless expression, maximum eyebrows, clasped hands and all that. Bobby smiled first at him and then turned toward me with that same charming, all-teeth alert. But I responded with a look that told him I could poke out both his eyeballs with my own two fingers – just jab right back all the way through the sockets. So Bobby dropped his smile, turned his head away and brought his foot up onto his knee. He started tapping his other knee. I couldn't help myself. I was staring at him out of eyes that were more like slits in the blinds of a film noir than eyelids. I wanted to pound him, to kick him as hard as I could, but then I thought, no, that's his game: pushing people around. I wasn't going to lower myself to that level.

"So you two are getting married tomorrow?" the counselor asked.

Bobby nodded, and I said, "Fuck, no."

Bobby leaned over. "Don't talk like that, Barbie," he said in a soft chagrined voice.

"What seems to be the problem?" the counselor asked.

I just glared at Bobby.

"I pushed her," he said.

"Into the refrigerator. My fucking rib is cracked," I said.

The counselor looked at Bobby with his eyebrows scraping his hairline.

Bobby stared into his hands and said, "It was an accident. I never meant to hurt her."

"Right," I said. I wanted to spit blood, but the anguish on his face was as real as his skin, and I had to admit, if only to myself, I wouldn't have fallen so hard if I'd been sober.

"Tell him what you did," Bobby said to me. I didn't say anything.

"She failed to mention the fact that she has sex with other men," Bobby said and stared at his loafer, going up and down, up and down.

The counselor turned to me with the same helpless expression.

"Only when I drink too much or do a lot of coke," I said. "Those other guys don't mean anything to me." I wouldn't have told Bobby, but I figured he ought to know what he was getting into.

The counselor looked as if he was trying to draw a word from somewhere miles away in his head. Finally, he said, "Why?"

He probably meant why were we getting married, but I pretended that he meant why do I screw men who don't mean anything to me and the answer was, "I don't know." I'm sure it had something to do with my alcoholic father who never gave a shit about me, but that always seemed a cheesy kind of reason to be as screwed up as I was.

The counselor rubbed his eyes. I figured he had scant hope for us, but he turned to Bobby and said, "If she stopped having sex with other men, would you promise not to push her or hurt her in any way?"

"I'll never hurt her again no matter what she does," he said. I glanced over at him. I was about to say, that's what they all say. But there was something intriguing about the light around his head, and I knew all that tough-guy Navy Seal business was only a facade for someone so gentle he could not kill a spider. Instead he would catch it in a shoebox and set it free outside. I realized I didn't want to be set free.

Bobby turned to me, and I floated like a lily on those blue eyes with the gold rings around the irises.

"Do you think you could give up these drugs and the drinking?" the counselor asked me. "Could you promise not to sleep with other men?"

Now I was the one searching for a word that was trapped somewhere back a mile or so in my head. All my life people tried to tell me what to do. And this is something I figured out early on: I don't like authority. But they were asking. Bobby was asking. In a moment the word came flying from the far dark recesses of my mind all the way to my lips.

"Yes," I said.

We were married the next day. My best friend Suzie was my maid of honor. We kept our promises, and I was glad overall, but lugging those promises around was like walking in mud – not impossible, but not all that much fun. Sometimes I thought they would choke me.

I went home and checked my voice mail, but there was nothing from Rip, and I already suspected there wouldn't be. So I started calling the better hotels in town – there aren't that many – and I found him. He sounded as if he had just woken up, said he was in room 403 and to come on over.

I started pushing buttons again and soon had my girlfriend Suzie on the phone.

"Let's go for a ride," I said. "Remember my friend Rip? He's in town. At the Hilton on the river."

"I thought you were getting too old for this shit," Suzie said.

"I just want to see him," I told her. "He's married now. He's got a baby, I think. I want to see how much he's changed."

"Can't you do that by yourself?" she asked.

"I don't think I should," I answered.

"Give me thirty minutes," she said. "I've got to take a shower."

I drank a cup of Hazelnut, looking out at the garden Bobby had created in the backyard. He had worked for weeks, making a brick patio where he placed a white wrought iron bench and a birdbath. He'd planted geraniums, Easter lilies, eranthis and Holland tulips that looked like red and yellow chalices. He left a section for the wildflowers that he knew I liked.

Bobby and I met at a party a few years after I'd

graduated from college. I was twenty-seven years old and tired of the circuit. Bobby loves to read and he was doing the philosophers at the time. He and I got into this long-winded argument about Nietzsche and that whole Dionysus versus Apollo thing. Eventually we discovered that we were the only ones left sitting around the pool. The other guests were gone, and the hosts were in bed. I reached over, took his wrist in my hand and looked at his watch. It was four a.m. I realized as I crawled into his arms that he could make me forget a lot of things. He did. I loved Bobby, but things had recently begun to change. My marriage seemed a lot like this garden with its rows of tulips. Safe and pretty and predictable.

Suzie came through the back gate. I opened the back door and stepped onto the patio.

"I'm ready," I said.

"No coffee or anything?" she said.

"It's after noon," I said. "Haven't you had your dose yet?"

"I wanted some of your hazelnut," she said. I went back in the house and came out with a cup for her. She took a sip, smiled her sly smile, shook the bangs from her eyes and looked around.

"How many people you think Bobby killed?" she asked.

"He never talks about it. Besides he's a trainer now. All that other stuff is history," I said.

"It's all history, girlfriend, all of it," she said, sucking coffee off her lips.

"Please, spare me the Kierkegaard," I said.

We went out the back gate and got into her black Camaro.

"Hey, where were you this morning?" she asked. "I called earlier. Were you at a meeting?"

"Are you kidding?" I said. "I haven't been to a meeting in a month."

"Me either," she said.

Suzie turned up the music – REM. She was reading my mind. There were certain REM songs that reminded me of wilder, if not better, days with Rip. For instance, the one that goes "I could turn you inside out." Actually, REM was kind of mainstream for Rip. His favorite bands were the Meat Puppets, Love Tractor and the Crucifux, though I think he might have liked their names better than their music.

"We were so depraved," I muttered. It awed me that I could have been that girl – the one who appeared at his apartment wearing only a jean jacket and blue bikini panties shortly after midnight. I'd driven from Jacksonville to Tampa where he lived then. We hadn't lived in the same city since college. I was famous among his friends as the Love Slave. Not very flattering (or original), but I didn't care what they said.

"So did you guys ever hook up? Like in a real relationship?" Suzie asked.

I shook my head.

"After college we saw each other maybe three times a year. More than that probably would have killed us. He'd get a quarter ounce. I'd bring my nose. One time we went to one of those medieval fairs – you know, with all the jousting and madrigals. We'd been up all night doing serious septum damage and all that goes with it. Everyone at this place stared at us like the sex and the sin was just pouring out of our glands. I didn't think we were really acting that strange, but people were watching us like we were part of the show," I told her.

"Maybe they thought you were going to be burned at the stake, and that it wouldn't be such a bad thing," Suzie said with her usual aplomb.

"Maybe so," I said and stared out the window as we pulled off the highway. There have been lots of guys I've partied with over the years. With Rip it was more. It was the almost daily phone calls, the way we knew whenever the other one needed someone to talk to, and some sense of shared pain that made us feel good, like stepping into really hot water. Whatever it was led us to push the rules back further and further each time we got together.

"Rip and I are the kind of people who need to be with people who will keep us from committing suicide," I said. "I'm happy he finally found someone who does that for him."

"Yeah," Suzie said, wheeling onto a side street. "You seem to be thrilled. Me, I just wish I could give them up. All men. Or just have one I could keep in my closet until I need him like a pair of pumps." Suzie wore a smoky quartz crystal that gleamed as she leaned over and looked down the road before rolling through the stop sign.

"I used to think masturbation was the key to a good life. The one thing you could do that would satisfy you and not demand any kind of real effort," I said. "But now I think that it's actually a dispersal of energy. Not good to waste it like that. Maybe that's why the Bible is against it."

"The Bible is against everything. Homosexuality even, like God would be against something that doesn't overpopulate the earth," Suzie said. "Have you read the Old Testament? Seriously, gang rapes are us. The Bible was written by psychos."

"I think the Ten Commandments were probably written by God," I said.

"Maybe. Thou shalt not commit adultery," Suzie said. We pulled into the parking lot at the Hilton, and she let a valet take the car.

The lobby was a polished marble museum of plants, couches and brass luggage racks. I was wearing jeans and a yellow pullover top – nothing fancy or sexy – except for this perfume that I didn't wear too much because it always seemed like I was naked when I wore it. I guess what I wanted was to know if anything of the old me was left. Rip had this ability to see right into me like I was a hurricane lamp; his eyes could ignite the dark liquid inside.

With Bobby I was different. I was the kind of woman you could take to dinner with your parents. I was the kind of woman who obeyed traffic laws, the kind of woman who did not have sex in a car, the kind of woman who wore a safety belt and a bra.

Suzie and I got on the elevator and made faces at ourselves in the mirrored walls. I was glad she was with me.

Room 403. Rip opened the door. I remembered the last time I saw him – two weeks before I married Bobby. We had lunch in Manhattan when I was visiting my sister and he'd had a job there briefly. We went to the museums, we sucked face on the subways and we drank White Russians until we puked. He hadn't met the woman he married yet. Today he looked like the same old Rip: longish, wavy dark hair – fine and unmanageable – pouty lips, tiny gold earring, hook nose, eyes deeper than coal mines. But something was different. Well, there would be something different, of course. He was married now, possibly a father.

"Hey, motherfucker," I said.

"It's good to see you, too, Barb," he smiled, sort of. The kiss that fell on my cheek was more like a whisper. Suzie followed me into the room. It was the usual mauve suite with a little refrigerator and a cabinet with a lock on it.

"You ladies like something to drink?" he asked.

Suzie and I looked at each other. This was one of those

moments when we were supposed to give each other support. We did. The wrong kind.

"Hell, it's my four-year anniversary. I might as well have a mimosa," I said.

"Not a good idea," Suzie said. Then she added, "Fix me one, too."

"No problem," Rip answered. He was his usual sweet, gentlemanly self. He always reminded me of Ernie on *Sesame Street* – accommodating no matter how infuriating he was. There was a gentleness in his voice that laced everything he said, all his jokes, even his criticisms. Everyone liked him. He opened the refrigerator and brought out a bottle of Korbel Brut and a couple cans of Bluebird orange juice.

"Four years married, Barb," he said. "You're doing good."

"I guess so," I answered as I took the hotel glass he offered me.

"You guess so?" he asked.

"Barbie is like the American people," Suzie said. "After four years, she's ready for a change in the administration."

"It's not that," I said. "I just don't think I'm right for him. He thinks I'm someone that I'm not."

Suzie gave me a disgusted look. She didn't like Bobby much, but it occurred to me that perhaps she didn't think my marriage was such a bad deal after all. She had never tried to talk me out of it. Rip made no comment. The TV was on – sports. That's all Rip ever watched.

"So what brings you to our little burg?" I asked.

"A print job for a generator company. *Très* glam, huh?" he said. We had all majored in communications but Rip was the only one who wound up getting an advertising job. I worked as the chief photographer for a weekly newspaper at the beach. Alvin worked for the city. Other key members of the corps were Biker John (now deceased) and Melinda, currently managing a florist shop in Orlando.

I turned to Suzie and said, "He looks like Mr Wall Street, doesn't he? You know, in college, he never even bought the textbooks. But he's the one making eighty grand a year."

"You were the brain," he said.

I laughed, "No, you were. Remember the present you picked out for that sycophant chick who was always bitching at us during production class?"

Rip smiled. Suzie raised her tiny eyebrows in expectation.

"Nipple warmers," I said. "He bought some nipple warmers for her. That obsequious little wretch."

"She wasn't that bad," Rip said. "Not after she got her nipples warm."

I laughed too loudly and too long.

"Where's Bobby now?" Rip asked.

"Training," I said. "He's in charge of teaching the new chumps how to fall out of airplanes and that kind of thing."

"Mr Tulip," Suzie said and smirked.

We drank our mimosas and Rip made us each another one.

"You sure have settled down, Rip. No jokes? No stories of your latest crazed adventure?" I asked.

His face did this funny little thing, a half grimace, and his eyes started roving around the room. I wondered if marriage was getting to him already.

"Look," he said and crossed the room. "I got some cool T-shirts."

He opened a box full of T-shirts and handed one each to Suzie and me. They were black T-shirts with huge green lizards wearing sunglasses on them. Suzie and I slipped them on. They were extra-larges – perfect. Suzie lit a cigarette and pretended to be a fashion model. I was laughing. When you don't drink much, a couple of mimosas tickle you in all the right places.

"Hey, Rip," I said. "Remember that time at the Ritz Carlton?"

He was sitting in a wingback chair next to the window, blue sky sweeping away the white clouds like giant dust balls behind him.

"San Francisco, right?" he asked.

"Yes," I said with a laugh. The sixtieth floor, my hands against the window, clutching the black belly of the night, Rip behind me, hands encircling my rib cage. The memory of that night was like warm smoke winding through my body.

Now he was just staring out into the daylight. Well, yes, some memories are better left in the dark.

"So, Rip," I said. "Is it true that you're a daddy?"

Rip nodded his head.

"OK. Like is it animal, vegetable or mineral? I mean, do I have to play twenty questions? Don't you have pictures or something like that?" I asked.

Rip nodded again. He got up and walked across the room ever so daintily. It was strange. I realized he was somehow more fragile than I had ever known him to be. He went to his briefcase and brought out some pictures.

Suzie took the pictures and I gazed at them over her shoulder.

"She's beautiful," Suzie said. "How old?"

"Ten weeks tomorrow," Rip said. There were about six or seven pictures in the group, and I looked carefully at each one. Yes, it was certainly a baby all right, with Rip's pouty lips, hook nose but with her own chocolaty-blue eyes.

"Rip," I said. "What's wrong with these pictures?"

"What do you mean?" he asked.

"There's no Mommy in these pictures," I said.

Rip stared at me. And then his face turned quizzical as if he had just remembered something odd.

"She had heart troubles that we didn't know about," he said. "She died a few hours after the baby was born."

At first I thought I was supposed to laugh, that Rip had made a joke in extremely poor taste. But the expression on his face that had been puzzling me was suddenly so clear. I'd seen it on the faces of people on TV, people who had just had their houses blown away by a tornado or who had been the survivors of a mass killing on a subway or in a McDonald's. I remembered it from my mom's face after the state troopers came to our house and said that my dad had slammed into an oak tree at ninety miles an hour and they were sorry but there was nothing they could do.

Suzie put out her cigarette and curled up in a ball on the couch. I sat down on the other end, and Rip came over, sank to the floor and put his head in my lap. I looked down at him and felt glass shattering inside my chest. I leaned over, and my arms slid around him. He clasped me tightly and I heard a muffled sound trapped in his throat. We stayed in this embrace for a long, silent moment. I ran my fingers along the fine black strands of his hair. I wanted to erase his pain, to squeeze it from him, to rip its claws from his neck.

I took him to the bedroom while Suzie stared at the television and pretended to watch downhill racing from Austria. Rip's eyes had gone soft and puffy at the edges.

"I'm sorry," he said.

"No," I answered. "Come here." We lay down on the flowered bedspread. I held him for a long time first and then slowly undressed him, pulling his shoes from his feet, releasing the buttons on his light-blue shirt, then on his dark blue Docksiders, and then pulling them off his thin limbs. He was quiet, submissive.

A friend of mine once said that screwing her ex-husband was like holding the head of a vomiting child. This was not like that. It was more like carrying a scared cat along a busy city street. He was clinging to me the whole time and I could feel his heart beating in a wild, unhappy rhythm. I stroked his head, his back, everywhere that I could reach. After we were done, he rolled off of me and we both lay there for a moment. I could smell the hotel sheets and the damp scent of our sex. He kissed my cheek and then slowly stood up and walked to the window. He gazed down at the river below.

"Who's taking care of your baby girl, Rip?" I asked.

Rip turned around and looked at me. His hand nervously fiddled with his wind tunnel-hair. His eyes were so dark, I could not see the pupils.

"She's with Elisa's parents. I'm staying with them for a while," he said. "I'm not really ready to be alone yet."

"Yeah," I said, pulling a pillow close to my chest. I thought about the way loneliness had chased me all my life, all the way up until the moment I met Bobby. Even with Rip I had been lonely. "I know what you mean."

Rip came over and sat on the bed beside me. I didn't know whether to reach for him or not. He had been my friend for so long, but I'd hardly seen him the past few years. It hadn't even dawned on me yet that I had done what I had promised I would not do. I mean, I knew what I had done with Rip, but I only knew it at one level, the level at which you wonder about the weather or what to fix for dinner.

Rip was staring into space.

"I wish you had known her," he said.

"Me, too," I said.

He gazed down at his hand. He still wore his wedding

band. Then he did something strange. He kissed the ring on his finger. The windows were closed but I felt a breeze. It was as if I had been standing in a dark room and someone had opened a door.

I reached over and touched his arm. He turned around, ran his fingers along my face and then looked into my eyes for the first time since I'd been there. I realized as I had often realized before that I was not in love with him. I had needed him, but I didn't know if I had ever loved anyone. A feeling of tenderness surged through me as if I was a conduit for the way his wife must have felt. It was a strange sensation and I felt a little dizzy.

After a while I got up, picked up my underwear and started getting dressed.

"I better get home," I said. "Will you be all right?"

"Someday," he said. Outside the sun was piercing through the clouds like one of those religious postcards, but my molecules were all scattered and white noisy and I couldn't appreciate the sight or even the irony of it.

"You gonna be OK?" Suzie asked when we got to my house.

"Yeah, I'm fine," I said.

"You didn't do anything all that bad," she said and pushed in the lighter not to light a cigarette, but just for something to do.

I didn't say anything.

She sighed and said, "I'll be by tomorrow. There's a morning meeting we could make."

"That would be fine," I said and got out of the car.

I walked inside the house. I couldn't sit down and so I wandered from room to room – kitchen, living room, den, bedroom, guest room and bathroom. Bobby would call in a couple of hours, and I couldn't imagine what my voice would sound like. Finally I went out into the garden.

Kneeling down in the middle of the flowers, I felt the dirt under the palms of my hands, and gazed at the flowers around me. I wasn't thinking about anything – just remembering the strange feel of Rip's arms tight around me and the love that wasn't mine but that seemed momentarily to wipe out the traces of who I was.

The fabric of the evening light curled softly around me. The Easter lilies smelled thick and velvety. A deep and voracious yearning slowly spiraled down from my skull into the pit of my being. It took me a moment to catch my breath. Then I wondered if I'd ever be satisfied, ever fill up the vast emptiness inside me. And what would my husband do if he knew, if I told him, that I was incurable, that no promise could bind me, that another woman's death served only as an excuse for me to drink at my poisoned well?

I sat there until the tulips drank the last drops of color from the day. Then I got up, dusted the dirt from my knees and went inside to wait for my husband's call.

Giving up the Guilt

I stopped thinking about him fifteen years ago. I closed the lid to that coffin and buried him. In my mind, anyway. Why talk about it now? I guess it's because we've become such good friends, and sometimes, I think you wonder why we can't be more than friends. There's this attraction that hunts us down in spite of all our good intentions. So I've been thinking a lot about this poison we sometimes call love.

When two people are meant for each other, nothing can keep them apart. They'll cross continents before they even meet, not knowing why until they have found each other. But when two people are violently wrong for each other, the attraction is unbearable. These are the two faces of love.

He and I met in a drug program. It was in a rundown old two-story house in a rundown neighborhood in a rundown town. We replaced our addictions effortlessly – from drugs to each other. His name was Roy. I'm not blaming him for what happened. He wasn't a bad person. Wasn't even really a drug addict. Alcohol was his problem. I think he'd had a drunk driving accident or something. He was middle class, about twenty-four, couple of years of college, wore polo shirts. Not a junkie or a criminal. I, however, was the real McCoy, four years on heroin, and that fascinated him, I believe. The way it sometimes fascinates you.

Within the first week of my stay at the drug program, I experienced my initial "house water fight". Roy chased me down, drenched me outside with a bucket of water and then hounded me into the dining room where he covered me in flour.

"Ow," I screeched, "you hurt me."

"Did I?" he said, kneeling beside me, his enormous jaw thrust out, his wide unearthly pale blue eyes full of concern.

"Well, not much," I said.

"Good," he answered and doused me with water again, grinning maniacally, mercurial soul. Mercury – also known as Hermes, god of the spoken word, thief, trickster – the one who came by surprise. We managed to find each other alone in odd corners of the house. How did we do it in that house full of people? How could those spies, those people with all their interest in our every move, not see the dangerous light in which we danced?

I remember one time, sitting outside, just the two of us in reclining lawn chairs, on the dirt beach, faces tilted up toward the sun. The whole damn yard was dirt. When a new person first arrived, they had to rake circles in the dirt day after day. This is part of the therapy.

By some chance, no one else was there except for a counselor, doing paperwork in the office. The rest of them had gone to a softball game. But Roy had a bad cut on his foot, and I was new and not allowed to go anywhere yet. We should have just gone into the girls' dorm in the small building behind the main house and screwed our brains out. We should have just gotten it all out of our systems. But we barely spoke. Instead we lay by each other on the lawn chairs, our arms a few inches apart, burning in the summer heat.

I had come into the program at 107 pounds. I'm 5′ 6″, you know. I looked emaciated, but within a few weeks, my jeans were too tight, bra squeezing the breath out of me, face round as a vanilla wafer. He and I began to joke about our weight. We were fat, we said, fat, fat, fat.

At the dinner table, I'm reaching for the milk and he says, can you get your chubby little fingers around the handle? He makes me laugh so hard, I piss in my pants or I spit milk out of my mouth. He turns me to liquid. I cannot convey the manicness of his humor to you, not in a thousand stories. But I began to feel insane I laughed so hard. And I wasn't alone. Everyone was attracted to his humor, his keen intelligence. He knew the latest of everything – music, movies, politics – and saw the inherent absurdity.

At the morning meetings, our eyes did not dare meet. Everyone else took it all so seriously, but he and I would be reduced to weeping in hysteria. Perhaps I wouldn't find him so funny now. I know that once we broke free of that environment, we did not laugh so hard. But that was later.

I ask you how can I be the person I am now – the person you know, who is honest and generous and hardworking to a fault? How can I be the person I am now and the person I was then? But I see I am repeating the age-old question and you want the story. You want scenes and dialogue. There is not much dialogue in the realm of madness where he and I dwelled.

I can tell you about the first time he told me in his

own weird way that he had feelings for me. He was assigned to the desk that night, which means he had to answer the telephone and log in the calls. We were listening to Super Tramp, *Breakfast in America* – is that the title? – something like that. One of the other girls was there, too, and one of the house cats sat in my lap. Roy was harping on me as usual about how gargantuan I had become, making sure he threw the sliding glass door open all the way when I came in. And I was laughing and trying to say how enormous his own bulk was. Actually, we were both about the size of normal people. Finally, Jennifer, the other girl, got up and left to make peanut butter and jelly sandwiches for all of us in the name of obesity. So then it was just the two of us. He began to stammer.

"There's something I wanted to tell you, fat girl," he finally blurted out.

"What?" I asked. I knew, but I wanted him to tell me.

He looked at me with those planet Venus eyes and then stammered some more. Then he drew two boxes on a sheet of paper.

"There's you and there's me," he said. I looked at the two boxes. Then he drew two more boxes but these were side by side. "And here's what I think is happening."

I stared at the piece of paper.

"But your box should be much bigger," he said. I swatted him, laughing, and Jennifer came in with the sandwiches.

Funny how love makes you deranged. All right, it's not love – desire, lust, infatuation. When it comes on you, you're febrile. If you really want to make damn sure two people go mad with desire, forbid them to fall in love. We were told when we entered the program that no relationships were allowed with each other in therapy. But

Roy and I were like a couple of vampires with our teeth stuck in each other's necks.

We touched each other whenever we could. When you are in the field of the erotic, even the smallest most innocent gesture becomes suggestive, laden with meaning. Don't you agree? I mean, even absently stroking the neck of a bottle of Heineken at happy hour like you're doing now begins to mean something when you are in that field. It's like mathematics. In different fields, different variables have different meanings. What is X?

You're looking at me. You do know what I mean.

One night we met by the side of the girls' dorm. We kissed, our whole bodies vibrating like a couple of hummingbirds.

Did you know that hummingbirds' wings beat 200 times a minute during courtship, more than twice as much as normal?

Anyway, he slid his hand into my jeans. And what he did with just his hand convulsed me, shot me sliding back against the wall, tore me away from myself and that world.

The next day a new kid – one I had "orientated", as they say in the TC, a week before – said he was confused. Here I had told him these rules about how you couldn't have sex with someone else in the program and that if you did you were breaking a cardinal rule, but then he saw me and Roy coming from behind the girls' dorm and what were we doing back there?

I looked at the new kid.

"I'm just supposed to tell you the rules. That doesn't mean you have to obey them," I said. He had this sour little disappointed look on his face, and I thought to myself that if they could get real junkies in this place it wouldn't be so bad.

The kid ratted on us. I had to wear men's clothes and a stocking cap on my head and clean the place from morning until eleven p.m. No one could speak to me. Roy had to sit on the bench. The bench was actually a milk crate, not comfy. He sat on it every day from sunrise to eleven p.m. while I cleaned. No one spoke to us. But the new kid and another kid – they were all kids except for a few of us – would go by me and sing that Lynyrd Skynyrd song "Oooh, that smell".

I ignored them. Hell, I didn't mind cleaning. Rather do that than engage in their pathetic therapeutic discourse any day.

In group that week Roy and I were finally allowed to speak. The counselor asked me why I got involved with Roy.

"Because he makes me feel special," I answered.

"Why don't you feel special anyway?" she asked. I didn't have an answer for her. Then she asked Roy what he thought he was doing, breaking a cardinal rule like that.

"You were sent to us by the courts, Roy," the counselor said. This was a woman I had grown to like. She'd been a junkie for twelve years. She was tough and funny and had crooked teeth. Before Roy and I got into trouble, she had once said to me, "You got this way about you. It's like you're reeling everybody in. Even me. What makes you so hard to resist?" I didn't have an answer for her. All I knew was that I wanted people to love me, and for some reason I destroyed them as soon as they did. Love was a disease as far as I was concerned. And I was like a carrier.

"You know, if you don't make it through this program, Roy, you could go to jail," she continued.

Roy looked down at his hands. Then looked up at her.

"I know," he said. "You're right. I don't want to go to prison for a cunt."

I was sitting on the other side of the circle with my

stocking cap on. I pulled the stocking off, and my hair fell down. Then I looked at him. I just looked at him, slowly sinking into myself, and at that very moment he died. I don't mean I planned to kill him. It's just that he evaporated before my eyes. I think she knew something had happened – the counselor, I mean. Like a tremor passed through the room, fate licking the envelope. The madness we had indulged in changed color.

After a while, we both got off contract. That's what they call punishment. In their therapeutic little minds, they must have figured they had effectively instilled enough hate in us toward each other that we would never again sneak off behind the girls' dorm or anywhere else. Got their lessons from Orwell, I guess. And we didn't. You wouldn't know we had ever been friends.

One day soon after, the whole house went to the beach. We all packed into a big van with the name of the drug house on the side. Once we got there, I wandered off down the thick shell-littered sand, away from the crowd. I felt the sun seeping under my skin like a narcotic. The noise of the surf droned hypnotically, quieting the words in my mind. What would it be like to just be a regular person, I wondered.

A guy about my age walked by me. Then he stopped and turned and followed me.

"What's your name?" he asked.

"Mellificent," I said. She had always been my favorite fairy in *Sleeping Beauty* – the evil one.

"Wow," he answered, and then he pointed to a two-story shingled house. "That's my parents' beach house. I'm visiting them, but they're gone right now. Want to come in for a beer?"

"No, thanks," I said. Drinking was against the house rules. "But I'll take a coke if you have one."

"Sure," he said, "Sure. No problem."

Inside the beach house, he took me downstairs.

"This is my mom's room," he said. It was a nice room, big bed with a pale blue bedspread, mirrored closet doors, a fresh beachy smell. I smiled at him. He had blond hair, wasn't great looking, wasn't ugly. I reached behind my back and tugged the string of my bikini top just once and it fell to my feet. Then we lay down on his mother's bed, our movements steady and rhythmic as waves.

I didn't tell the others about the guy in the beach house and his mom's bed even though it was perfectly all right for me to have sex with someone who wasn't in the program. To be honest, I don't believe I've ever told anyone about him before. It's one of the most pleasant little secrets I've got, like a favorite marble that you take out and roll between your fingers. The time I slept with a total stranger for no reason except for the pleasure of a man's body on mine. But it's not a secret anymore, is it?

A few nights later, Roy became a "splitee". That's drug program terminology for someone who leaves the program before finishing it. Before he left, he walked into the girls' dorm and found me lying in bed, reading a book.

"I know you don't care about me anymore, Frances," he said and handed me a slip of paper. "But this is where I'll be staying if you ever want to get in touch with me."

I looked down at the address on the paper, folded it up and tucked it into my book. For a moment we looked into each other's eyes. He was like a bottle full of pain. Then he turned around and left. I figured I would stay on. As far as I knew, I'd go to jail if I left. I had a case – prescription forgery – still pending in Valdosta, Georgia.

But damn if I didn't let those kids bag me again. A week later one of them gave me a joint. I don't even like marijuana. Never have! But this kid gives me a joint, and the old junkie in me just cannot turn him down. I sneaked out back, took about two tokes, and then I got paranoid, went inside and flushed it.

As soon as this kid had given me the joint, he went upstairs to the counselors and ratted me out. "Giving up the guilt" is what they call it. If you do something wrong, you won't get in trouble if you go tell on yourself. That's something I could never bring myself to do – tell on myself. Seemed like the stupidest thing a person could do. At least up until now. Is this what I am finally doing after all these years? Giving up my guilt? And to you?

You know I used to be a vegetarian – after all this happened, of course. Then I started craving meat. I asked this yogi guru what to do, and he said, "The only thing you can't swallow is guilt." Now, here I am, sitting at this bar with you, eating a hamburger, ketchup dripping down the side of my mouth. I'm sorry. I got off track. The upshot is that they held a big guilt session, and I got in trouble again. As a matter of fact, they told me to get out. She did, the counselor that I liked so much. "Get your shit and leave, Frances," she said. I didn't argue with her.

I had my grandmother's old car there at the program, just gotten it as a matter of fact. But I didn't know where to go. I couldn't go back to live with my grandmother in Orlando. I'd caused her so much trouble. It was hard enough on her when my mother died, and I didn't want her to know that I'd gotten in trouble – once again.

I found Roy in a studio apartment in an old house downtown. He seemed thrilled to see me, but we were both awkward and kept drinking to dispel our fears. By midnight, he and I had drunk two six-packs of Old Milwaukee and were side by side in his bed watching Johnny Carson on a black and white TV.

The next week is kind of a blur. But I remember the highlights of our pitiful crime spree. We went to my hometown of Fort Lauderdale and broke into the condo that my dad kept specifically for dates with hookers. We weren't worried because he was out of the country with my step-mother. We had no money, so one day we went into a Winn Dixie and filled a cart with beer, crackers, Chips Ahoy, cheese, bread, more beer, bologna, cans of Vienna Sausages and tuna. Then we walked out of the side door and into the parking lot. What a foolproof and delicious bit of larceny it was. Then one night we went to the best seafood place in town and ate lobster and drank a bottle of champagne which we nearly puked up as we ran down the street with the waiter chasing us and screaming at us for slipping out without paying.

What did we do when we weren't committing these petty crimes? Well, I'll tell you what we weren't doing. We weren't having sex. All that heat and passion, gone. He couldn't do it, and I didn't want to. At first I was frustrated, but then I realized that I didn't care. I didn't care about anything at all. I just wanted to get fucked up. And nothing seemed to work.

"We need some serious drugs," I told Roy.

"Francie, we can't even afford beer," he said. We'd been watching TV all day and had started drinking some of my dad's Cutty Sark.

"Let's rob a liquor store," I said, finally. "We'll get you a wig, I'll buy a gun. You can do it."

I remember the way Roy looked at me, as if I couldn't really mean it, but I had told him about guys I knew in Orlando who robbed places and got away with it. He looked like somebody standing on the edge of a cliff, almost convinced that he can fly.

"You can do it," I said again.

We sold the TV to buy a gun. I wish it hadn't been so easy. So easy and so stupid. You'd think he would have had the sense to say, it's your idea, you go in and rob the man. But he didn't. If he had, then nothing would have ever happened. Somehow he drank enough whiskey to get himself nerved up. We should have waited until it was late, but we figured if we did it early enough, there'd be some traffic and we wouldn't stand out so much speeding back down Sunrise Boulevard.

I stopped the car behind a dry cleaner's next to the liquor store. Roy got out. He was so nervous he kept pulling his wig off and then putting it back on. I have never seen anyone so scared of anything in my life. But he finally walked away and around the building to slip into the side door. It was a drive-thru liquor store, and we figured he could just sneak in behind the counter and rob the guy without anyone seeing. We had cased the place and choreographed every move Roy would make. It would take no more than two minutes, we figured. If it took longer, he should just bag it and split. I waited until he disappeared around the building.

While I waited I remembered the counselor back at the drug program asking me why didn't I think I was special. It was like someone else took over me as I slipped the gear shift from neutral into drive, pressed down on the gas pedal, and left him.

I drove clear across town and put the rest of the money from selling the TV down on a cheap motel room. I went in the room and double-locked the door. I was nervous. I was sure somehow he would find me and kill me for leaving him. Though of course there was no way he could find me. He barely even knew the town. I forced myself to turn on the television and lie down on the bed. I wanted to jump up every time I heard footsteps in the hallway, but I wouldn't let myself move.

Finally, the eleven o'clock news came on. A man had robbed the drive-thru liquor store on Sunrise Boulevard west of I-95. "The suspect fled on foot," the reporter said. The police caught him running through the parking lot behind a nearby shopping center and shot him six times. The reporter stood in front of the liquor store beside a cop car, lights still revolving across the scene of yet another Friday night tragedy.

I turned off the television and went to sleep.

After a while I washed him from my mind like cleaning the smudge from a dirty window. You wonder how I could forget about this, you with your eyes incredulous and green as the summer. I can't tell you.

Did I pay for what I did? How can you pay for someone's life except with your own? Eventually I got busted for a rather low-level felony. I went to prison, served my time and came out the reformed citizen that you now know. Finished college, got a job and immersed myself in my work. No better hiding place than the catacombs of a multinational corporation, right?

Come on, let's go. Back to our offices with their splendid views of the city and comfortable chairs. Call your wife and tell her how much you love her, send her red roses, buy her some of that perfume she likes so much. Tonight my husband and I will fix dinner together. That's one of my favorite parts of marriage, cooking together. I mix a salad and make bread while he fries a fresh fillet of fish. After we eat we'll sit on the couch, feet touching, and read our magazines or watch television. My favorite shows are cop shows. You know, the good guy always wins.

Purple Haze

The year was 1970. I walked along the middle of a red clay road, red dust swirling around my toes which poked out from my long Indian print skirt. I also had on a black shirt that I'd shoplifted from a five and dime in Valdosta. Black was not proper attire for July in Georgia, but it was all I had.

Campfire smoke lingered in the thick, moist air. The sky looked like a bucket of blue paint, and the tall pine trees seemed sure to wilt at any moment. I passed vans tucked along the road in the woods, and tents and other people walking slowly or sitting in the shade. A tidal wave of heat dragged me forward.

I was hungry. My stomach felt like it was plastered against my backbone.

A tall, naked man stumbled toward me, his penis dangling like a deflated windsock.

"Acid, acid," his voice sang out.

My eyes slammed toward the dirt below my bare feet.

No one else seemed to notice him. Everyone at the rock festival was older than I. They uncovered their bodies without shame, showed nipples, curls of pubic hair and underarm hair and soft white or brown haunches. All the women were beautiful with long braided hair, bare feet and blissed-out smiles. There are a million years between sixteen and fourteen. I couldn't forget that, though I tried.

And I was hungry.

I kept thinking of the Mexican family we had stayed with in Fort Myers – the warm tortillas awash in butter, the beans spilling across chipped plastic plates. I hadn't trusted the guy who took us there, and yet his mother had fed us, and his little brothers and sisters put on a play in Spanish for us. But that was days ago.

I kept walking. I'd been down to the creek to wash off. I'd taken off my skirt, but nothing else. Everyone else shucked down bare nude, but I couldn't stand the thought of them seeing my little-girl body.

I saw a small stand on the side of the road. A chick with stringy blond hair, wearing a tie-dyed halter top and cut off shorts, sat behind it, selling corn on the cob. In the pocket of my skirt, I had just enough, just enough for one piece of corn. I walked over and handed her my last fifty cents. She gave me a piece of corn, wrapped in tin foil. It was warm like a living thing in my hand. I unwrapped it greedily and ate as fast as I could.

"They said on the radio it's 104 degrees in the shade," she said. Her skin was darkly tanned, almost bruised-looking, but it was probably just dirt. I was afraid to speak, afraid of my soft voice. I should not have been there at that rock festival. I did not belong. But even as the corn slid down my throat, I was glad I'd come. I knew I would have stories to tell for the rest of my life. I could already picture myself at school the next year, telling my friends about all this – the blanket of reefer smoke, days and nights of music, the naked guy on acid. Then it occurred to me that I might never go back, never see my friends at school. And if I did go home, surely I'd never be allowed back at that school where the dean went to rock concerts to see if any students from our school were there smoking cigarettes.

I'd been away from my home for almost a month, having left right after school got out. I had told my mother I was going to spend the night with a girlfriend, but instead I started hitchhiking south with an eighteen-year-old draft dodger that I'd met at the park by the river where all the freaks hung out and sold or bought nickel and dime bags of pot. I'd packed a blue overnight bag with an extra pair of jeans, a toothbrush and every pair of clean underwear that I owned.

Our first ride was in the back of a pick-up truck filled with watermelons. The watermelons were green and fat, and the summer air, thick with sagging grey clouds and interspersed with shafts of gold light, adored us. I watched the road spool out underneath us and thought that freedom was an emotion like fear or joy, and I was feeling it, really feeling it for the first time. I had smiled at the draft dodger, and he smiled back.

We went to Daytona Beach, hung around the boardwalk for a while. I fell in with some nuns helping runaways while the draft dodger searched for some of his friends. By nine, he was back and we headed to a crash pad in an upstairs apartment in an old wooden house. People came in and out. They were friendly, all love beads and peace, reading *Trout Fishing in America* and burning incense. I felt as if I had joined the company of the gods, but I could barely overcome my shyness to speak to anyone. In my other life, I was not particularly shy. In fact, I had performed in a Lillian Hellman play that spring, playing the role of a malicious girl who starts a rumor about her teachers. But my whole life framework had the insubstantiality of a stage set. It was learned lines for plots that made no sense. I had dismantled it in a day.

At the crash pad, we smoked pot at night, ate black beans and rice and listened to the Rolling Stones' *Let It Bleed* album over and over.

"So you heard about the Midnight Rambler," my draft dodger would sing in a falsetto and gyrate across the balcony.

After a few days we went to the beach with a surfer in a Valiant and another guy. The surfer had blond hair to the middle of his back and scars on his legs from where he'd gotten hit by his board, I guess.

"Here, try this Panama Red, little chick," the surfer said and handed me a glowing doobie. I took a hit, lay back in the sand and burst into laughter.

"What is it?" the draft dodger asked me.

I pointed at the clouds and said, "Turtles."

Everyone else looked at the clouds and started laughing, too. We passed the laughter back and forth like a baton in a chaotic relay race. Finally we got so hungry we headed back, riding in the surfer's old Valiant, Jefferson Airplane wailing from his 8-track.

When we got back to the skinny two-story house where we were staying, a chick with small eyes and hands on her hips met us on the porch.

"She has to go," she said, pointing to me with her chin. "The pigs came by, said they heard we had a runaway here."

I stuck my hands in my pockets. I felt as if my mother was just a few steps behind me, calling out my name with that worry wrapped all around it. She was the bane of my life with that worry of hers, lurking at the periphery of my vision.

So that night we slept in the back of someone's station wagon. The draft dodger and I cuddled together, and he planted wet kisses on my lips. He was skinny but it felt good to have his bony arms around me. I'd never had a real boyfriend before. And having one helped me forget about what this adventure was doing to my mother. I tried not to imagine coming home, finding her back in the hospital as if she could call the cancer back at will. It took all my willpower to build a fortress thick enough to keep her watery eyes out of my head.

I had told people that I just wanted to see the world, to go some place I'd never been before, to immerse myself in what was left over from the 1960s and do something exciting. When one of the nuns who fed me that first night in Daytona Beach asked if my home life was bad, I said, "Not really." I guess I was like my mother in that respect, thinking it was not too bad to have an alcoholic haunting the house as long as he didn't beat up anyone. I did have a lock on my door, so he never crawled into my bed and did the things alcoholic step-fathers may be prone to do. I truly believed it wasn't unhappiness or the rage suppressed in every cornice that I was fleeing, but experience that I was running toward.

The next day we decided to go to Canada and caught a ride as far as Gainesville where we stayed in a log cabin with a couple of college students. One of them showed me how to make the Indian-print skirt. I'd lost my extra pair of jeans, and the ones I was wearing were stiff with sweat. She was dark-haired, wore gold-framed glasses and told me that someday everything in life would be free – electricity, food, a house for everyone. Then she loaned me a copy of *Valley of the Dolls* and I read it voraciously.

Pills, beauty and death – they all fell together like pieces of a child's wooden puzzle.

"Capitalism," she told me.

Life, I thought.

The draft dodger decided to forget Canada, and I was secretly glad. I wanted to call my mother, but knew that the sound of her voice would be like a lasso around my neck. So I called a girlfriend and told her to tell my mom I was all right.

"When are you coming back?" the girl asked.

"I don't know. Maybe never," I said and hung up quickly.

The next day we met the Mexican guy who took us to Fort Myers, and we slept on the living room floor of his mother's apartment. They lived in a small purple apartment building with about a thousand other migrant farmers. The kitchen smelled dazzling as a palace. His mother kept petting me on the head, whispering *bonita*.

Then we headed toward the highway again, started hitchhiking. We slept that night in the green grass by the interstate. I'd had no idea how cold it could get at four in the morning even though it was summer. The draft dodger, all bone, body odor and skin, could not warm me.

That morning a car filled with people, tents and sleeping bags stopped for us. We crammed ourselves in. My draft dodger had one of the easiest smiles, and people liked him right away.

"Man, y'all gotta come with us," the driver said. "We're going to a rock festival. Big as Woodstock."

And then the draft dodger said he knew the reason we hadn't gone to Canada. We were going to go to a rock festival in Georgia – big as Woodstock.

"Fuckin' A," the driver said.

After I ate the corn on the cob, I found the tent where we'd been staying with some of the people who brought us – a guy and two chicks. They nodded but didn't have much to say. They were stoned, and moving in this humidity was like wading through chocolate syrup. I didn't know where the draft dodger was, so I sat down against a pine tree and wished I had something to read. I'd gotten turned on to T.S. Eliot at school the year before, but really I read anything – Conan books, sci-fi, Tolkein. I'd even read *Candy* about this stupid chick who screws anybody and though it had made me seem worldly on the volleyball court, I knew it hadn't really taught me anything.

I dug my hand into the pine needles. The house where I lived when I was a little kid had pine trees like these in the front yard. I remembered playing tag and hide-and-go-seek with the other kids in the neighborhood, lost until dusk, my mother having forgotten about my very existence as she played her violin in the one air-conditioned room in the house. This was before she'd gotten remarried, before she and Richie bought the big house where everything including the trees got cancer, except Richie who became an alcoholic, drinking Smirnoff straight from the bottle.

It was well into the afternoon before the draft dodger ambled down the lane toward us. I thought of him as the draft dodger, perhaps in deference to the Artful Dodger. I was Oliver, always wanting more.

"Where were you?" I asked, trying to sound curious rather than worried. It had occurred to me more than once that he could leave me as easily as he'd found me. I was sure worry helped drive my original father out of our house. I didn't know what made the next one turn to drink.

"I was at the stage, man. They got one for smaller

bands down that way. Man, some bitchin' bands were playing," he said, nodding his head, still hearing the music whirling around his skull.

"Oh," I said. "You want to go back?"

"Naw, no one's playing anymore."

I shrugged, combed my fingers through my hair.

The draft dodger was scruffy-looking with his crooked teeth and dirty hair, but smiling. He was gentle and young, and I could see why he didn't want to go to Vietnam. He leaned toward me, and I could smell the campfire smoke in his hair.

"I got some acid," he whispered, "for free."

I held out my hand, and he gave me a hit of purple microdot. I'd taken mescaline before – a mild hallucinogen. The one thing I knew was that it cured hunger almost immediately. At first I didn't feel much of anything. I waited for it to hit while we walked around the various camps. People were selling things we of course couldn't buy – handmade bongs, beads, leather goods. I started feeling sick to my stomach. Sounds kept coming from the wrong direction.

By the time we got to the edge of the woods, I had lost all my boundaries. I could feel molecules floating away from my skin and then falling back into place. Then time leapt forward with nauseating speed. The next thing I knew I'd been dropped into a huge field, surrounded by half a million people. I was amazed to be around that many people, to smell them in the heat, to see them lying, sitting, all with long stringy hair, a hundred shades of skin, most everyone in jeans – a weird free-floating mass of energy. I could almost touch it, a big silky net all around me. People walked over me, around me. They passed joints. They drank beers or cokes, whatever, dropped empty cans to the ground. They flicked lighters. They kissed.

As an enormous jet cruised just above the field, half a million people said in unison, "Far out." And in a moment the daylight disappeared. I looked at the stage. I wasn't sure, but it looked like a purple ferris wheel. When I lay down, the ground began to turn as if we were on the top of a large screw boring into the ground, and I thought what a fabulous thing for them to do – whatever geniuses had planned this. I had a sense of the universe as a gigantic clock. And it was ticking, ticking, ticking.

Then the crowd started chanting, "Jimi! Jimi!"

The draft dodger looked at me. His teeth had purple violin strings attached to them.

"It's Jimi," he said, his voice warped and sounding like a tape at slow speed. "Jimi."

Jimi Hendrix sauntered out on the stage, lifted his guitar and sent sharp spears of electric music zinging past our ears. "The Star-Spangled Banner". I told myself that this was history and I was living it. But I didn't feel like I was living it. I felt as if I was watching from the other side of a plate-glass window.

Everything was purple, the sky, the dirt below me. Then someone sidled next to me and reached for me. I turned and stared into the purple face of some older guy with oily skin who was touching my hand and my leg and asking me to come stay in his tent with him.

I edged closer to my draft dodger. But he was lost in his own echoing reality and he didn't seem to care that this man with his grizzly pointed chin and his dirty teeth was grinning at me and that his wormy fingers wouldn't leave me alone.

"Go away," I said, surprised my throat still worked. "I don't want to go to your tent with you."

I stood up and headed back toward the campground.

Fuck Jimi, I thought. I waded through the swaying sea of people and finally made it to the paved road and across to the dirt road. The purple pine trees sang the same phrase over and over: "Oh, say can you see? Oh, say can you see? Oh, say can you see?"

I was just a little kid, I realized, but I wouldn't be if I weren't a virgin. I walked and walked but nothing changed. I decided I had probably walked into another dimension. If the universe was a clock, it could be many clocks, and I was pretty sure I had stepped through the hands. I would never find the tent where the people from Florida were staying.

I stood at the edge of the clay road and saw a van parked in the woods. The side door was open, so I crawled inside. I lay down and watched the purple trails that my fingers made.

"Hey, what are you doing here, little chick?" someone asked me.

I looked up and knew that I had reached the acid's magic for there was the lanky surfer from Daytona Beach, and his voice was full of delight, his eyes like the eyes of a very old wise man. I laughed when I saw him, and he smiled back at me. Of course, I didn't have to say anything. He came into the van with me and shut the door behind him. He pulled off my shirt and unbuttoned my skirt. As he peeled off my underwear, his arms and belly grew thick fur, and his incisors became long and pointed. I thought about a fairy tale I loved as a kid – *Beauty and the Beast*. I remembered the pictures of the Beast in a garden full of roses. My own arms were like rubber-bands and my hands could stretch out for miles. My skin melted into his as he pushed himself between my legs. A thousand tiny noises battered my ears, and his grunting was like the sound of an animal eating.

In the morning I woke up very early. He lay beside me, snoring. My legs were sticky. I slipped out from under the arm draped over my back and put on my clothes quickly. My underwear had disappeared.

I took one last look at him, and then I had to close my eyes hard. I opened them again and stared. I'd never seen that face before. He had no scars on his pale legs. His hair wasn't even blond. My tongue felt like a brick inside my dry mouth. I decided never to remember his face, and I got out of the van. What I would tell people later was that I gave my virginity to a werewolf one night.

Outside the world was a fractured marble. The sun was beginning its onslaught, and the humidity washed over me like a tongue.

I had a sudden memory of my mother before she had cancer and lost her breasts. I saw her smiling on the other side of a sheet that we were both holding. The sheet smelled like white air. We raised the sheet high and then let it fall on the mattress. We tucked the sheet around the corners of the bed. Then I lay down on the sheet and rolled on it, laughing.

As I stood outside the van, I wanted more than anything in the world to feel her arms around me, to bury my head against her ruined chest.

I found our campsite, but the draft dodger was not there.

"I think he's over in that yellow tent," someone said. So I went over to the yellow tent. I looked inside, and the draft dodger was lying naked with the girl who sold me the corn on the cob. I wondered what kind of animal she'd been the night before. A hyena probably. The draft dodger looked up at me. Then he glanced at the naked girl beside him. He rubbed his belly.

"I want to go home," I said.

"All right."

"I mean, home. Back to Jacksonville."

"I know what you meant."

The traffic leaving was a continuation of the party, moving five miles an hour along the one road out. People hung out of car windows and threw Frisbees to each other. But my mind was acid-frazzled, and all I wanted was a bath and some food. Some real food.

Early that evening they dropped me off at the base of the highway leading to the Fuller Warren Bridge. I climbed up the green embankment to the street. They were on their way back south. The walk to my house was a few miles, but I didn't even think about it. I just walked, carrying my little bag of clothes.

Maybe a block away from my house a cop pulled up beside me and asked me where I was going.

"Home," I told him. "I'm going home." There must have been something about the way I said it that made him believe me, and he drove on.

A few minutes later I walked through the gate and up the steps of my house and knocked on the door. My mother opened it. She looked ten years older than when I left, shoulders slumped and hair gone gray and flat. I wondered for a second if I was at the right house.

"Dear God," she said.

"I'm tired," I said. She stared at me, and I felt like I was looking at one of those prisoner of war pictures that was on TV sometimes. Neither of us could move. Finally I went inside and she shut the door behind me.

She looked as though she was going to collapse, but she didn't. I tried not to look at her. Instead I glanced at the parquet wood floor, the large gilt mirror hanging over the little table in the hallway, the stairs leading up to my bedroom. It was the same old house, and I was glad to be back but not really.

"Where's Richie?" I asked.

Her mouth moved; nothing came out.

I didn't know what to do. I knew she wanted to tell me what I'd done to her, how I had almost killed her. But she couldn't find the words. I knew that her love for me was like barbed wire twisting around her heart.

"He's gone to the store," she finally said.

"I'm going to take a bath, OK?" I said.

Her eyes looked tired and so frightened.

"I'm not going to leave again, I promise," I said. Then I went upstairs and I drew a hot bath. Warm air floated in through the open window. The tiles in the bathroom were black and white, the fixtures old, glass doorknobs on the cabinets. I poured some strawberry bubble bath into the water and then got in. My body had two small breasts, a sparse growth of pubic hair. I ran the bar of white soap down my belly. It felt as if I was washing the whole world off me.

In a few minutes I heard the door downstairs open. He was back. I could hear their voices, mumbling. Then his footfalls on the stairs. The door to their bedroom closed. I looked at the white bathroom door with the red towel hanging from the hook in the middle. I sank down and let the silent water close over my head.

The Deep End of the Blue Sky

We put a hospital bed in the living room for Daddy to die in. My mom had turned the back half of her house into a one-bedroom apartment to make some extra money, but the last renter had moved out leaving hair dye all over the bathroom walls, a busted water heater and a hole in the floor of the bedroom. Mom said Daddy could stay there as long as he needed to. He had sold his own house before we left for New York. There was nowhere else for him to go.

The first day back, I put clean blue sheets on the bulky hospital bed and cranked open the windows while Daddy's friend Chip took him to the drugstore for steroids to keep his brain from swelling. It was spring, and a dogwood molted white feathery blooms onto the ground outside. Cardinals had built a nest in the chinaberry tree near the windows. I thought Daddy would like that. People called him Birdie because he built birdhouses as a kid. When he grew up, he built people houses, but the nickname stuck.

Daddy couldn't move his left side and so he had to lean on me and his friend Chip to get from the car into the house. We were his crutches.

"Y'all are doing good," he said, "really good."

"I'll build a ramp for a wheelchair," Chip said.

"Fine," Daddy said. "But I'll be walking soon. Wait and see."

I believed him. For one thing we never thought he'd make it this far. He was supposed to have died that day in the hospital in New York, but three days later Daddy and my mom and I were all on an airplane on our way home, Daddy clutching my hand the whole way. Mom held onto my other hand. We were like a chain. About halfway through the flight, tears began pouring down Mom's face. She hadn't cried so much since their divorce six years earlier.

Mom had been ready to shoot Daddy before we left because he'd taken me out of school to visit his girlfriend Lily and to make the rounds of the modeling agencies. Daddy said I was a sure bet for Calvin Klein. I'd been begging him to take me to the city ever since Lily had moved into a brownstone apartment and started taking art classes at NYU, which Daddy paid for. Daddy told my mom that high school was a waste of time. Not only that, it was oppressive, "a killer of creativity." Mom said Daddy didn't live in the real world and he never had. She insisted that I stay home. We left anyway. For two weeks we visited the museums, had picnics in Central Park, saw movies and plays and even got an appointment with someone who knew someone at the Ford agency.

Then everything went way wrong like a birthday party that ends in a shooting.

Before he got sick, my daddy was tall and blond with blue eyes the color of the water around Bimini. He ran five miles every day. He never smoked cigarettes or took drugs though sometimes he drank a glass of Courvoisier with Lily. Then one morning I went into Lily's bedroom to wake him. Lily had showered and was toasting bagels in the kitchen. Daddy wasn't asleep. Instead he sat up in bed, staring down at his hand.

"I can't move it," he said. The words slurred out of his mouth as if he was eating mashed potatoes and talking at the same time.

"What?" I asked.

He looked up at me with a confused expression on his face.

"I can't move it," he repeated in that strange, drunk-sounding voice.

"Lily!" I called out.

"It's probably a stroke," Lily said a few minutes later, ransacking the Manhattan phone book for a walk-in clinic. "People survive them all the time."

At first we didn't know what to do. Daddy didn't have insurance and never had trusted doctors much. It took the three of us the whole morning to remember that as a veteran he could get free care. He'd been an infantry platoon leader in Vietnam. He'd killed for his country. He still cried about it sometimes, the moaning he and his men heard all night after an ambush, only to find a little girl's corpse in the morning with half her guts missing. You wouldn't think that was something you'd forget, but none of us was thinking too clearly.

When we took him to the VA hospital and they did an MRI, the doctors discovered a brain tumor the size of a plum. They operated the next week, but when the doctors came out of the operating room, they looked tired and disgusted. We stood in the hallway outside the ICU, Lily and I did, as the main guy tried to explain how the tumor, a glioblastoma, had sunk tentacles like hooks into the depths of Daddy's brain.

"There's absolutely nothing we can do," he said. He looked at me with bloodshot eyes and said Daddy might not make it through the night. I felt myself falling back against the wall.

"What the hell do you mean?" Lily asked the doctor. "What the hell do you mean?" He didn't have an explanation for her.

I found the payphone and called Mom.

I was eight years old when Daddy taught me how to see the universal field. He sat me on a bench he had built out of oak in the backyard and told me to stare out at the trees around us. He pointed to a large live oak. I looked at it. I saw brown bark, thick climbable limbs and moss tinted yellow with sun.

"Don't think of it as a tree," he said. "Don't think of it as a thing. Just see it as an 'is'. It's this whole idea of names that has people so confused. Everything just is."

I looked at the oak, then I stared at a sky-soaring pine, and then I looked at our black cat slithering through the dark green monkey grass.

"The cat is just an is, too. Look down at your feet. You're part of the is." He was laughing when he said this. I laughed, too.

Maybe because I was only eight, I somehow understood what he meant. There was no separation between me, the cat, the tree or my dad. Later I went back to my regular way of thinking except from that day on I never felt completely apart from my dad. I never tried to keep a secret from him – even after the divorce, when I split my life between my parents. We talked about everything: religion, politics, my boyfriends, sex.

"Look around you," he said. "Sex is everywhere. Nothing would be here if it weren't for sex. Sex is life."

For the first few weeks, Daddy seemed to be himself except that he spent all his time in the hospital bed. In the mornings I drank Kukicha tea with him before going to school. Chip usually came by before I left to take care of him in case he needed anything. Chip had fixed the hot water heater with Daddy's guidance and nailed some plywood over the hole in the bedroom floor. Chip and Daddy had been running partners. Chip would show up in his running shorts with a sheen of sweat on his skin. He had his own business so he could set his own hours.

"We miss you out there," he'd tell Daddy.

"I'll be back," Daddy said.

Every day different people came by to see my dad. Some of them were cheerful. Some of them would break down and cry. Women cooked macrobiotic foods for him, saying cancer lives on sugar. Some of the women had been his lovers. Daddy was gorgeous, but said no one could own him ever again – not even Lily.

Aunt Julie arrived a week after we came back. Julie lived in Miami and had driven up as soon as she heard the news. She stayed in my mom's half of the house and spent hours calling doctors around the country, trying to find a cure for my dad.

Mom came every evening after work and had dinner with us in the apartment. Sometimes she'd stay with Daddy if I was going out with my girlfriends. I don't know what they talked about, but her eyes grew hollow as if she was draining herself, pouring out the things she'd held in all these years. Daddy smiled at her and watched her as she moved around the room, picking up newspapers and books or gathering up dishes. I could feel something smoothing out between them, but I kept out of it.

One weekend, Mom and I painted the bathroom walls a bright turquoise color. We painted the cabinets purple and yellow. Daddy sat in a wheelchair and watched from the doorway.

"Paint a palm tree on the wall, Sweet," he said. So I did. Then Mom took some white trim paint and painted a bird flying, and then I painted some droppings coming from the bird, and a little stick figure under the droppings. The three of us started laughing. I knocked over a can of paint and we laughed even harder.

I slept in the bedroom or on the rattan couch in the living room. Most nights Daddy and I watched movies from the video store. His favorite was *Pretty Woman*, which neither of us had liked before he got sick but then I guess we both needed a happy ending no matter how ludicrous.

"You're beautiful enough to be in movies, Sweet," he told me. He always told me I was beautiful. My daddy never lied. I would look in the mirror and see his blue eyes looking back at me. But now when I looked at him I saw a bald head with a scar and gaunt cheeks. He'd lost his looks pretty quick. I thought it might bother him, but it didn't.

One night I was feeding him the macrobiotic soup that one of the women had made. His eyes watched me, his mouth open. A strand of seaweed slipped from his mouth and hung on his chin. He'd grown a beard. I scraped the seaweed with the spoon and edged it into his mouth. His eyes smiled.

"That's good, Sweet," he said.

That night while we were watching Richard Gere help Julia Roberts buy some non-slutty clothes, Daddy had a seizure. His fists clenched and his legs went stiff. The blue of his eyes rolled back where I couldn't see them. I held onto the metal railing of his bed and called his name, but he wouldn't answer, wouldn't look at me. My mom wasn't home, so I grabbed the phone from the little basket by his bed and called Chip. Then I ran out of the house and stood outside in the backyard and tried to breathe.

Squares of yellow light from the house fell across the gray-green grass. A dog in the next yard barked frantically, and a small twin-engine plane overhead beat the warm black air. I remembered Daddy saying one time that the spiritual masters all emphasized compassion as a path to understanding our oneness, but I didn't feel compassion. I only felt alone. I was dissolving, and the sounds of the night moved through me as if I was made of smoke.

When I came back in, the room smelled sour and dark. Chip was wiping off Daddy's backside with a washcloth. Daddy looked over his shoulder; his eyes met mine. Their color had faded. He smiled weakly. I knew I should help, but instead I went into my room and turned out the light.

The next morning I sat in the grass outside the house, ripping clover out of the dirt with my fingers, tears and snot smearing my face. The sobs came like blows from deep in my lungs. A shadow darkened the grass. I recognized the shape of my Aunt Julie.

"What the hell are you moaning about?" she asked.

"What do you think?" I asked and threw some grass.

"You had sixteen years. Sixteen years of a father who worshipped you. God, do you know how many times I almost died of envy watching the way he treated you? We didn't have that. He and I. You had love. We had brutality."

Aunt Julie took a deep breath.

"That doesn't stop me from being sad," I said. "I have a right."

"Oh, we all got rights," she said in a dry voice. I hated her so much I wished she were the one dying. She didn't have any kids. What difference would it make? No one would miss her. Her red-brick voice continued.

"I never got a present from my father. Nothing for birthdays or Christmas. One time when I was ten years old, I was taking a bath, and the bastard came in the bathroom, dragged me out of the bathtub by my hair and threw me out the front door. For no reason. No reason at all. It was 34 degrees. I was only ten years old, and I was naked and wet. I would have died if Birdie hadn't knocked him out of the way and let me back in the house. Ten years old. Can you imagine?" Her voice faded.

"It wasn't Grampa's fault," I said. "He was mentally ill." But she wasn't listening to me. She went right on talking.

"You've had it so good. Too good. Birdie never raised his voice, only saw the good in you, your shit smelled like rose water. He sold his house and took you to New York so you could try to be a model. He'd do anything for you – anything. God, what I wouldn't give for just one day of love like that."

The sobs that had gathered in my shoulders gradually subsided.

"No wonder Birdie's got a brain tumor. All that ugliness we lived with has come back to kill him," she said. Then she sucked in her breath loudly, and I realized she was stifling her own sobs. I didn't know if she was heartbroken for Daddy or for herself. That evening Aunt Julie drove back to Miami.

At school my friends didn't really know what to say about Daddy dying. They all knew him, all liked him.

He'd helped us with art projects and driven us wherever we asked him to when everyone else's parents were too busy or too tired. He was the cool dad. I didn't know what to say either. So we didn't mention it. We talked about guys, gossiped about our teachers, and mostly focused our attention on our favorite Ska band, a group of local guys who called themselves Breech Birth. None of us ever thought about the future. College, careers, marriages – that was Martian territory, too cold, no oxygen.

At the end of May, Lily showed up. She shooed the macrobiotic women out of the house and fed Daddy lasagna, beer, spaghetti and meat balls, ice cream.

"For God's sake," she whispered to me in the kitchen as she poured butterscotch syrup over the speckled vanilla bean ice cream, "give him what he wants. Whatever he wants."

"He's not going to die, Lily," I told her.

She nodded and said, "I know that."

Lily and I went shopping at our favorite thrift store. Lily was like the sister I'd never had. She was much younger than Daddy. She'd lived with him for two years before going to New York. I guess leaving was the only way she could break free of him. Not that he ever held her back, she told me, but he was just so easy, so comfortable.

"I'd never grow up if I stayed with him," she said, trying on a pair of black suede trouser boots with silver studs. "Should I get these?"

"They're only ten bucks. Of course you should get them," I said. "Do you feel grown up now?"

"A little. Maybe I was wrong to go to New York," she said as we walked out of the musty-smelling store without buying the boots. "I could move back here."

"He'll be fine," I told her. "Wait and see."

But the next few weeks the tumor took my father piece

by piece. He slept more and more. He forgot people's names. Even when he was awake he could sometimes be gone. Like he'd call someone on the phone and then as soon as he'd hung up, he'd call again and again like he was stuck in some kind of automatic loop. Then a few hours later, he'd be normal, cracking jokes. He'd say, "If you want to straighten out all your relationships, get a brain tumor."

One Saturday afternoon as Lily and I sat in the living room playing a game of Continuo, Chip and his wife came by to visit. They sat in the two rocking chairs and talked to Daddy.

"We were bickering last night, Birdie," Chip's wife said. "I was so mad at him. I told him I'd rather live in the Apalachicola National Forest than live with him."

"Well, you were the one who wouldn't admit you were wrong," Chip said.

Chip's wife was a tall woman with red hair that swirled over her shoulders whenever she tossed her head, which she did a lot. She crossed her arms over her chest and looked away from Chip.

"Be grateful for that bickering," Daddy said to her softly. "Be grateful."

Nobody said anything for a minute. Then Chip's wife nodded, uncrossed her arms and said, "I am."

It was the closest he ever came to admitting that he was dying.

My mother and Lily passed by each other more like aircraft carriers than ships in the night. They did not register on each other's radar. I never really understood their animosity. Mom had a boyfriend of her own, a smart and funny guy, certified as a serious catch among my mother's set, who owned a restaurant in town and took her for sailing trips in the Caribbean, a boyfriend who came over and helped bathe Daddy or carried him to the bathroom when he needed to go. And Daddy had had other women all his life. Maybe it was just that Lily's and my mom's love for him was too big to both fit in the same small space.

A few days after Lily's arrival, my mom came into the apartment.

"Melissa, I need to talk to your father," she said.

"Come on, Lily," I said.

"Why do I have to leave?" Lily asked.

"Come on," I said. She got up from the big recliner by Daddy's bed and followed me out of the house. We took a walk to the park down the street and swung on the swings in the playground. A few kids were running around us, throwing dirt at each other.

"I wish I could have had his baby," Lily said. I didn't say so, but I was glad she didn't. I didn't want him to be anyone else's daddy. Just mine. Forever. I could almost feel his hands gently shoving my back as I swung high towards the deep end of the blue sky. I slowly stopped swinging.

"I can't live without him," I told Lily. "If he dies I'll die, too."

Lily scratched a mosquito bite on her arm and didn't say a word. I was glad she didn't try to comfort me. When we went back, Mom was leaving with a folder full of papers.

"His finances are such a mess," she said as we stood together on the porch. She reached out and ran her fingers along a strand of my hair. She started to say something, but when she opened her mouth nothing came out.

Lily decided to shave her head. Most of Daddy's hair was gone from radiation treatments that hadn't worked.

I guess she wanted to be like him. We went into the bathroom, she sat backwards on the toilet seat and I took the pair of scissors she handed me. The scissors made a *shink, shink* sound as I cut the thick ropes of her long black hair. I cut it shorter and shorter. When it was not even an inch long I covered her skull with handfuls of lime-smelling shaving cream. I took Daddy's razor and made swipes from the front of her head down to the base of her neck, from one ear to the other. I nicked her once but she didn't flinch.

"I'll never cry over a little bit of blood again," she said.

That night Lily slept next to my father, his good hand cupping her newly bald head – a couple of eaglets in a nest of sheets. I went to my room. I couldn't sleep. I couldn't think. I just stared into the black space behind my eyelids until finally morning came. I got up and stood at my window as the light trickled onto the blue surface of the sky. Clouds began to take shape.

I had saved Lily's hair in a basket. I dug my fingers into it, brought it to my nose and smelled it. It was dead, but it still carried her scent. I dropped the dark strands back into the basket. I got dressed in my jeans and a yellow tank top, went into the living room, kissed my father on his bald head and headed to school. The air outside had a quiet feel. For a moment I forgot that my father was dying.

That afternoon Daddy wrote a check for five thousand dollars to Lily so she could go to Paris.

"Don't stay here," he said. "Go now."

When my mom heard about the money, she went out on to the back porch so he wouldn't see how mad she was. I followed her.

"He doesn't have the money, Melissa. We may have to get private care for him. He made some terrible investments, and what about your college? I can't afford it on my own. Lily doesn't think about anyone but herself. I just can't believe this," she said, balling her fists and pounding her thighs.

The dogwood was no longer in bloom but the crape myrtles glittered pink as princesses. How could everything be so lovely, I wondered, without my father to witness it. All my life, everyone had told me how lucky I was. One time a couple of girls at school cornered me in the bathroom and told me I was spoiled rotten and conceited. I'd laughed in their faces and said they were jealous. Now I could see that it was true. I'd always floated a few feet above the hard ground. I couldn't be touched. Until now.

"I don't care about college, Mom. I just want my daddy," I said.

My mother put an arm around my shoulder.

"I know you do, baby, I know," she said.

The night Daddy died, my mother and Chip and I were in the room with him. Aunt Julie had returned, but she had fallen asleep in my bed. Daddy had been unconscious most of the day, but around midnight he opened his eyes. I sat next to him on the bed. He took my hand. Then he kissed the back of my fingers once, twice, three times. He kept kissing, maybe twenty or thirty or fifty times, before finally his lips stopped moving and he closed his eyes.

Chip stood up and opened the windows. Then my mother teetered into Chip's arms. I ran my fingers over my daddy's chest. His bald head lay tucked against his sunken pale chest. He had lost his beauty and lost his intelligence, two things he had prized so highly in himself and in me, but what had been left was infinitely more precious.

We had a memorial service in the backyard. Aunt Julie and all his friends came and told stories about him and laughed and shared little things he had written or said or done. I didn't say much; it wasn't required. I could have told them that he'd set me free like a bird from a golden cage but I didn't think they'd understand. I wasn't sure I really understood – it was more like a feeling than something I could put in words.

After everyone left, I sat in a wicker chair on the front porch of my mom's house. Evening spread itself over me like a silk blanket. A mockingbird chased a crow across the sky. My mom's cat lay on the railing of the porch with his front paws curled into his chest. He blinked at me sleepily. I watched the world before me for a long time. I watched until I couldn't remember the name of anything.

Picture Day

It is picture day at Wal-Mart, and my neighbor, Beth, and I are going to get pictures taken of our babies. I am planning to send one to Jack's parents to show them the grandchild they have never acknowledged. Melanie is crying with hunger, and the phone is chirping at me. Instead of ignoring the phone, as I should, I answer it.

"Hi, Holly."

"Gerald," I answer, juggling the crying Melanie. Gerald is a copy-editor at the newspaper in Miami where I used to work before I had a baby, before I moved to Tallahassee for graduate school. His is the third long-distance phone call I've gotten this morning. I sit down in my Goodwill rocker and open my blouse for Melanie, who greedily lunges for my left breast. I'm always amazed by that fierce little shark attack and then her tiny firm hands holding my breast as if it were a big white hamburger.

Gerald is despondent over his life, and it's not exactly

the kind of conversation that one can politely end, saying "Look, I've got to go to Wal-Mart," so I listen and commiserate.

"I'm so depressed," he says. "Leonard is in South America on a trip down the Amazon, researching the effects of deforestation with federal grant money while I'm putting commas in obits. Even you're better off."

"It's harder than I thought it would be, Gerald. My neighbor says she'll show me how to get on the WIC program – free cereal and cheese," I say. As my baby drinks from my breast I'm thinking about the day, shortly after I became pregnant, that Jack told me I had to choose between him and motherhood. His brown eyes, which had always been so full of laughter, had turned hard as brass. I push the thought from my mind and stroke Melanie's pumping cheek.

"I want to face the elements," Gerald says.

"Day-to-day survival can be an adventure, Gerald," I tell him. Melanie is wet, and I don't know what she should wear for the pictures. Most of the dresses given at my baby shower are too wide for her.

Gerald finally hangs up. Between his call and the two others, I have spent an hour and a half on the phone. And Melanie is now ready for her afternoon nap. Will I ever get to Wal-Mart? I put Melanie in her playpen and hurry to the apartment next door. Beth says she'll be ready in about twenty minutes and lends me a couple of dresses for Melanie.

When Beth comes over, I have Melanie dressed in a pretty hand-made yellow and white dress and little yellow and white socks. I nearly strangle her snapping a bib around her chubby little neck so she won't drool all over the dress. Beth is a large woman with clear skin and cheeks as pink as watermelon meat. She is so pretty, I think, with big liquid eyes and dark haircut, short and full. She's a good thirty pounds heavier than what television has dictated to us as acceptable, but she carries it well, like one of those Hawaiian queens of the past, sexiness spilling from every pore. Her husband, Raymond, is muscular and his skin color is a deep, chocolate brown. Beth calls little Shanda, a rambunctious mocha baby with a head full of soft curly black locks, her "half-n-half."

"Melanie has such pretty white skin," Beth says. I don't tell her that I think the government should only allow people to have mixed babies like Shanda, that I think the result is so much nicer than either race originally is and that we'd all be better off with a combination of genetic characteristics. I guess I'm a reverse-Nazi like the inside-out sock on Melanie's foot, small as a snail.

We go in a caravan to Wal-Mart. Beth and Shanda in her car, Melanie and I in mine, and Raymond following in his car. At Wal-Mart we all find good parking spaces and head toward the doors. Raymond never says anything to me, which is fine. I prefer husbands who mind their own business and do not try to be my friend just because their wives are.

"Why didn't he ride with you?" I ask as we pass the yellow and red mechanical rocking horse outside the store.

"Because he's only staying for the picture," Beth answers. "He doesn't want to go shopping with me. I hate him."

We enter Wal-Mart and an old man holds the door open for us. He has been hired just to do that, to be friendly and old and to nod his head at us like one of those dogs that people used to put on the back dashes of their cars. Wal-Mart is like Oz, so cavernous and crowded. I always expect the shoppers to break out into song and the workers in their snappy red vests to leap onto their stations and kick up their heels in some Bob Fosse-style dance routine.

We pass the little restaurant and then the women's clothes – flowered shorts, turquoise dresses, yellow T-shirts, all cheap and bright and new, almost magical. I'm tumbling in a kaleidoscope of color and fabric.

The photographers have set up a little studio in the middle of Wal-Mart next to the lingerie section, and a crowd of people are there, most of them with babies or little kids. Good grief, I think, Melanie will never last this long. We put our names on the long list and take the babies down to the infant section to do some shopping. Shanda begins to fuss.

"Take her down to automotive and show her the automotive parts, Raymond," Beth says. Raymond wordlessly removes Shanda from her stroller and wanders away. I grab a bag of cloth diapers, not because I am the great environmentalist (though I wish I were). I just think they might be cheaper in the long run.

Melanie stares up at me with flying saucer eyes as if it is the first time she has ever noticed me. "What are you looking at?" I ask with a laugh. But she just keeps giving me that look of utter amazement, and a sharp little stab like a steak knife at my heart reminds me that if I were to disappear and be replaced by someone else, she would ultimately not know the difference.

Beth and I gather with the others and watch people get their pictures taken: a young man in an Air Force uniform, a brown-toothed woman with a wooden smile, and two scowling teenage girls who get their pictures taken together. I look around at the rest of the crew and think, here we are, people with nothing better to do than wait in Wal-Mart for hours. Again, I acknowledge the fact that I am now a member of the poorest group of people in America: single mothers. I am in my element here at Wal-Mart, but I'm not sure I'd rather be anywhere else. My "element" doesn't question my ringless finger, the absence of a husband.

Two women with a little red-headed girl about seven years old and a skinny little baby boy sit in the only two chairs. The baby boy is cute, and I'm glad to see another skinny baby. Melanie always looks a little puny next to Shanda who is two months younger and at least eight pounds heavier.

"She's so cute," one of the women says about Shanda. They don't have to tell me that Melanie is cute. I know she is beautiful. I have seen the way people stop and stare at her, surprised by the perfect childlike features on her infant face. Anyway, I am wandering around in the underwear section, just overhearing them. I should buy some new underwear, I think. What if I meet someone? I can't fall in love with anyone while I'm still wearing Melanie's father's soft Jockey briefs which are so much more comfortable than those silly little nylon bikinis I used to wear. One of these days I'll get some new underwear, but I'm not really worried about the possibility of a man undressing me any time soon. Maybe never again, I think.

I drift back over to the wait area. Only four people ahead of us now. And somehow I am in a conversation with the two women who have the only two chairs. One of them has oily hair in a ponytail and holds a baby boy. The other has short curly hair and is wearing a blue, terry-cloth, one-piece outfit, exposing most of her legs. She has a long red scar on her chest, and my eyes travel to it whenever we speak. I imagine her cut open by some angry boyfriend with a broken beer bottle in his hand. Then I notice another scar running along the inside of her leg. Her skin folds in toward the fresh pink line. Perhaps she was in a car wreck, or maybe her mobile home caved in during a tornado. I have a scar like a horizontal zipper from my C-section hidden by Jack's old underwear, another reason I may never make love again. I cannot bear the thought of a new man running his hand across that ridge and asking, "What's this?" But I rather admire this woman who wears her scars so proudly.

"Your baby reminds me of Althea when she was just a baby," she says, nodding to the little red-haired girl who is twirling in circles by the boys' T-shirts.

Melanie has been angelic, riding on my shoulder while we wait. The woman with the scars takes her friend's baby boy and follows me back over to Beth. I'm thinking about Jack and wondering if Wal-Mart sells guns.

"I can't have any more children," she says. "I had a heart attack last April."

She has snapped me out of my self-absorbed pool of pain like a yoyo. I have never known anyone who had a heart attack, and she doesn't look much older than I am. I tilt my head attentively, and she loves it. This is real-life Geraldo. Her little girl, Althea, play-acts a heart attack on the sidelines.

"I had open heart surgery," she says. "See this scar?" She holds out her leg, and I pretend I had not noticed it before.

"What's that from?"

"It's where they took a vein from my leg."

She has declared open season on herself as far as I am concerned, and I pepper her with questions. Where was she when it happened? What did it feel like? Where was the pain exactly? And lastly, boldly, I ask, how old she is.

"Twenty-nine," she says, and she had the heart attack at her mother-in-law's house and the pain was not that bad in her chest, but her left arm hurt real bad.

"They misdiagnosed me at first," she says. "I'm still trying to decide whether to sue. The problem is I really like the doctor."

None of us have any advice for her on that issue. Finally, miraculously, it is Melanie's turn to get her picture taken.

"I only want the package," I tell the photographer. The poor woman has been working without a break for hours.

"You have to take all seven poses," she says, "even if you're only getting the special."

"Well, I don't want the picture in the washtub," I tell her. I have already seen one little girl in all seven fakey-looking poses. The photographer drapes fake fur over a wooden triangle where she props up Melanie. "And I don't want the forest background. The plain blue will be fine."

"All right," the photographer says. "You sit here and reach through the back like this so you can hold on to your baby. Is she tired?"

"Yes." But Melanie maintains the poise of a beauty queen and grins toothlessly at the woman as she steps back and snaps the photo. Melanie smiles delightedly in every pose; I think she has made the photographer just a little bit happier, even though I have not.

"Please sit in the chair, Mother," she says crossly when I get up to see what Melanie will look like. I sit obediently. But then I behave badly again after the pictures are taken and her partner tries to sell me some hideous faux-gold charms: a necklace, a key chain and some other revolting facsimile of jewelry. I may be poor but I'm not ready to be tacky, too.

"We have a special on these charms, and if you don't get them now, they won't be on special when you come back, and if you decide you don't want them, you can just use the money towards the pictures," she says, all the while I'm shaking my head. The special on the pictures, by the way, is $4.95, but they try to dupe people like me into buying the deluxe package for $125.

"No, thanks," I answer.

"It's only $6 for three of them. Should I put you down for three?"

"I'm not interested," I tell her.

"How about if I just put you down for two for one," she says and starts writing.

"I swear to you. I swear I do not want a charm."

"OK," she says, sullenly. "We'll notify you when your pictures are ready." I cannot help but wonder if my order will mysteriously get lost.

I go to the toy department while Beth gets Shanda's picture taken and I pick up a crib mirror for Melanie. It's ten dollars and comes with a chime. I can't really afford it, but I want Melanie to be able to look at herself in the mornings. One of the magazines I've read said that all babies like this. I guess I am a dupe after all.

Shanda's lips curl downward as if she is disgusted by the fake fur next to her skin, outraged that it isn't mink or at least velvet. Beth laughs behind her hand and rolls her eyes at me as I come back to the picture booth. The photographer gives up; they got two smiles out of Shanda and that's all they will get.

"Morrison!" the photographer reads the next name from the list and Beth and I gather up our purchases to leave. Scar woman stands up and then looks around.

"Dammit, where is Althea?" She limps as she tramps toward the toy department.

On the way out, I ask Beth if she's going to give her parents one of the pictures.

"Are you kidding? They don't even speak to me anymore. It's the race thing." Ah, yes.

"I am going to send a picture to Jack's parents," I tell her.

"Do they know about her?" Beth asks.

"I sent them a letter, but they never responded. He probably told them she wasn't his." I picture them in their Nevada ranch home, doting on their legitimate grandchild, the son of Jack's sister. They never even called to see if she came out all right; they couldn't even be bothered to send her a lousy little teddy bear. I suddenly realize that I am clenching my jaw again. Relax, I tell myself, petting Melanie's bunny-soft hair.

As we leave the cool air-conditioning of the store, we hear a child crying and both of us look at our babies to see who has let loose her grief of the moment, but Melanie is sleeping and Shanda just smiles at Beth. The crying gets louder, and we notice a couple of frightened and confused little boys standing by the mechanical rocking horse which is gyrating with mechanical menace. On the horse, head thrown back and tears spilling off her cheeks is the little red-haired girl, Althea. We approach slowly.

"She can't get off," one of the boys tells us.

"It won't stop," the other adds. Althea sobs in rhythm with the rocking horse; she looks like a little lost cowgirl. Beth kicks the rocking horse, but that does no good. I try to hold its head and that doesn't work either.

"One of us is going to have to lift her off," I tell Beth. Althea's sobs subside momentarily, but now she has the hiccups. I hand Melanie to Beth and climb up on the platform of the rocking horse. Althea's face is a mosaic of freckles and tears; her brown eyes are the eyes of all frightened children. For some reason I want to laugh, but instead I insert my hands underneath her arms and pull her up as far as she will go. Her weight, the solidness of her body surprises me. She smells like grape bubblegum and I can feel her blood pumping as her hands reach for my shoulders. Her legs are too long, so I tell her, "Raise your legs, sweetie." She does, and I am able to bring her up over the broken bobbing beast and sort of drop her onto the sidewalk. She sniffles once and staggers a little.

"You better hurry if you want to get your picture taken," Beth says to her, handing Melanie back over to me. Althea says nothing, but after a moment she runs back inside the store. The rocking horse continues its frenzied pace.

Back at the apartment complex, a cheap place built about twenty years ago, Beth and I stand at our doors fumbling for our keys. A chinaberry tree rustles in the breeze. The babies are tandem fussing, complaining to each other in their own language about what terrible keepers we are.

Beth squinches her eyes and says to me, "They're such babies." We both laugh, wave goodbye and go inside.

That night after I put Melanie to bed, I sit at the table and write out checks. After about five bills are paid, I realize that there is just enough for rent, but nothing left over for food. I am going to have to go down to the county health unit and see whether or not I can get on welfare. My eyes are tired from staring at my checkbook and willing the figures to come out differently.

I go to my rocking chair and stare out the window into the black night. At the time I left my job at the newspaper and came up here to graduate school, it seemed the right thing to do. I didn't want to put Melanie in some daycare place from two in the afternoon until midnight. When would I see her? What would have been the point of having her? I thought the assistantship at the university would be enough, but I'm going to have to come up with something more from somewhere. Asking Jack for money was out of the question. He said he would move to another country before he would help me out. I feel like Althea, trapped on a machine that won't let me off. I stop rocking, get up and go to bed.

That night I dream that I am in a crater at the top of a mountain, and it is beautiful. The air is nice and cool and the sky is dark but then I try to get out of the crater and I can't. The cool air becomes cold. The dark oppressive. I try to scream for help, but my throat is empty.

Melanie's grunts and whimpers wake me up. I hear the chime on Melanie's crib mirror and wonder what she is doing. She couldn't have figured the chime out by herself, so I get up and go to the corner of the room where I've placed her crib.

In the soft glow of the night light, I can see the watercolor clown that my mother painted for her, and I see that Melanie has fishtailed around the crib and is kicking her mirror. I move her body and stroke her cheek. She quiets down instantly.

"Melanie, how are we going to make it?" I ask. Her answer is a soft dreamy sigh, and I bend over to let her warm smell baptize me.

As I stand there holding on to the edge of her crib, studying her blemishless body, I begin to wish that I could unzip myself and tuck her back in me, protecting her there forever. But I know that she had to come out. Someone had to save me. And in spite of the fact that I have no money and no husband, I have never felt the world so solid beneath my feet as I do standing beside the crib, watching this tiny pearl that is my child.

The Hurricane Dance

Sheryl was drinking a cup of black coffee in a thick porcelain mug with a picture of a dolphin on it when the phone rang. She reached over with one hand and plucked the receiver from its hook.

"Good morning," she said, glancing at the rooster clock on the wall of her kitchen. It was ten minutes after seven.

"Not really," answered Bill Caton, a deputy whose voice she recognized instantly. "We got a dead horse on Highway 12. One of the Corolla herd."

"Shit," Sheryl said, setting down her coffee. "What happened?"

"Car hit it. The driver's OK, but the horse flew ninety feet. We're over here by the Food Lion if you wanna come down," he said.

"Yeah," she answered, glancing down at herself in T-shirt and underpants. "I'll be there in ten minutes. By the way, was it a male or female?"

"A teenage girl. She's crying up a storm. I've called her parents to come get her," he said.

"I meant the horse."

"Oh," he said. "It was a stallion." She closed her eyes. The coffee began a tingling burn up into her esophagus.

After she hung up, Sheryl went back through the cluttered living room with its black furniture covered with throws and up the stairs to the bedroom. Zeke slept soundly under the yellow and white quilt, his dark hair poking out in tufts, his face stony with slumber.

She found a pair of cut offs on the floor and dug through a drawer for a bra, which she finally found hanging from the door handle of the closet. Should she wake Zeke, she wondered, or just leave a note. No matter what she did, it wouldn't be the right thing. Fuck it, she thought, I won't wake him or leave a note. It's a free country.

She got into her old Pinto, and thought maybe she should go back in. Zeke would want to know about the horse, but it would take too long. She scratched the back of her neck sleepily, cranked the engine and drove across the sound and over to the barrier island. The horses' territory was at the north end of the island. They would be safe if they'd just stay there. And most of them did now that a fence had been built clear across the island from the ocean all the way to the sound.

She drove past the strip malls, the hotels and the cheaply-built condos. Even the expensive "community" on the sound side looked bleak to her. Zeke was always coming up with crazy plans to drive the developers away.

Finally, past the village of Duck she found Bill Caton by the side of the road.

The car – a Camaro – was crumpled like a discarded beer can in the front but an airbag had kept the girl from any harm. Sheryl stared at her – a sheath of white-blond hair, dark eyebrows and braces on her small teeth. The girl batted blue eyes at Sheryl and said, "I didn't see him. I didn't see him. Not until he was right in front of the car."

"I know you didn't," Sheryl said. "It's not really your fault. It's the damn tourists who stop and feed them. We spent six hours yesterday telling them not to do it. The horses don't stay up north where they belong, keep coming down through that shallow area, thinking every car that drives by is gonna stop and give them a carrot."

Bill Caton crossed his arms, arms which looked like he spent too much time in a gym when Sheryl really knew his muscles came from hauling shrimp as a boy. He had a big blunt head and the buttery tidewater accent of the Outer Banks. He had been the one to call her a month earlier when another horse had been killed – that one by a family in a Dodge minivan on its way back home to Ottawa. She had cried in Zeke's arms for an hour after that one. No more crying, she decided.

"You people are gonna have to figure out how to keep them horses on the north end of the island. He went right around the fence on the sound side. You can still see his hoof prints on the beach," he said, leading Sheryl to the dead horse.

She bent down beside it, saw the blood trailing from its cracked skull, the thick lips still wet with saliva, the eyes mercifully closed. She thought of a story she had read in a book of mythology about a man in ancient Wales who had sliced the lips off his enemy's horses and thereby caused the ruin of two kingdoms. "The horrible things we do," she muttered.

She softly ran her fingers over the bones of the horse's forehead and through the coarse brown mane. He was one of the young ones. She didn't think he had even sired a foal yet. Her organization tried to keep a census of the horses without disturbing them too much. She wanted to lay her head against the felt platform of his neck. She never got this close to them except when they were dead.

"Animal control is on the way over," Bill said, his voice gruff the way men get sometimes when they are trying to be gentle. Sheryl held out her hand and Bill helped her up.

"I thought that fence would keep them from coming back down here," she said. "We need money, Bill. Money to buy some more land for them."

"Good luck," he said. "Land here only goes for condos – 'Sawgrass Hills' or 'Pirate's Haven' or some other dumb concoction. The tricks they pull these days. They're gonna kill this place."

The clouds had gathered in the sky, keeping the sun from its usual onslaught. Sheryl was glad. Flies had already started to buzz around the dead horse.

Sheryl drove past the Currituck Beach Lighthouse. The brick wall took on the flat tone of the sky. It wasn't painted white like most lighthouses. This spot was where the tourists sometimes stopped to look at the wild herd, direct descendants from the Spanish mustangs that came here whether by shipwreck or abandonment no one knew for sure. The tourists and the red-nosed children complained of the heat and the stickers until they saw those horses. Nothing like the sight of them really, wild like that. It touched a weird sort of erogenous zone inside the heart.

Sheryl drove back over the causeway and pulled into the circular dirt drive of the wooden house where she and Zeke lived. It was said that the house had been a hospital during the Civil War. Of course, all you needed to make a hospital then was some place to amputate wounded body parts. Zeke sat outside in the plastic lawn chair in front of the goldfish pond that they had made last year out of a kiddie pool. He had made a pump so that water flowed up over an upturned log and down through large conch shells. The goldfish swam seductively above the algae-coated bottom and a family of small black water frogs clung to the side of another log with watchful round eyes.

Sheryl sat in the other chair beside him.

"You don't have to work today?" she asked.

Zeke shook his head. He wore only an old pair of shorts. He looked fragile in a way with his ribs showing like the wires of a birdcage.

"Where were you?" he asked finally.

"Another horse was hit," she said, "killed on Highway 12. I went down to see which one."

He was silent. Sheryl wondered what it was that had seemed to lurk between them lately. This gulf that neither of them would cross.

"I'm thinking of creating a special dance," he said, finally, scratching his belly and gazing up at the laurel oak above them. "A hurricane dance. One that will smash all the hotels and the beach houses and that fucked-up new development that's sucking all the water from the island. Then no one will come here and the horses can have the whole damn place to themselves. The turtles can, too."

"But how would the horses survive the hurricane?" she asked.

"Not all of them would," he answered. "But enough would. Enough to start up a new herd."

"I don't think I like it," she said.

"You don't like anything," he said.

"I like you."

"You used to like me."

She didn't answer. He was right. She didn't like him as much as she used to. She thought of the nights when they'd gotten up to go move turtle eggs or stand watch to keep them safe from people who would trample on them or purposely smash them to crumbly slimy bits. She remembered the thrill of watching baby turtles head toward the ocean, Zeke's hand gripping hers as they lay in the sand quietly – their breath as light as feather strokes.

It seemed like everything died, no matter how hard you tried to protect it. She saw again the mustang's body, his legs cocked up underneath him as if he were still running in the fields of heaven. People couldn't really appreciate what was right before their eyes. She felt Zeke sitting beside her, holding back from her. Maybe he hadn't really seen her in a while. Maybe she hadn't seen him.

The thought sprang up like the water bubbling up from Zeke's fountain: this didn't have to die. They'd had this relationship for five years. And it was the one she wanted for at least another five – hell, maybe longer, if she really thought about it. Who else would understand the part of her that was connected to those horses, to all things untamed? She glanced at him, the long nose, eyes in a thickness of lashes staring ahead.

"You think I don't like you?" she said. She stood up and pulled the T-shirt over her head.

"What are you doing, Sheryl?" he asked, sitting up, his nipples dark and the black hair on his chest seeming to make the sign of the cross.

"I'm showing you how much I like you," she said. "I'm doing the hurricane dance."

She unhooked her bra and flung it over a branch.

"You're nuts," he said. He looked around at the roadway just beyond a crowd of bushes. A car passed, but did not stop. She slid out of her shorts and out of her underwear and then she stepped into the middle of the goldfish pond. Zeke stared, fish-mouthed. Then he got up, grinning and shucked his own shorts.

"Do you think anyone will report us?" he asked.

"Bill Caton won't put us in jail, sweetheart. I'll just say I'm grief-stricken. Or maybe they'll bill us as another tourist attraction – The Wild Humans."

She began wiggling her hips and waving her arms in the air.

"Come, oh mighty storm, blow through here like ancient Cronos swallowing his children. Bring on the Cyclops, bring on the Titans. Eeeeya, eeya, eeeee," she wailed. Zeke started to skip around the pool with its pictures of mermaids and seahorses. The goldfish swirled like worshipers at the new monoliths that had appeared in their midst.

"Your legs are like Stonehenge," Zeke said, stopping before her. "And you are the mighty Earth Goddess."

"Bow down before me, lowly one," she commanded.

Zeke stared at her. His eyes were the color of the algae at the bottom of the pool with flecks of yellow in them like goldfish scales. Then slowly he knelt and held his arms out toward her.

And she knew that life had nothing to do with happiness. That she would have to fight for the lives of the horses and she probably would not win, that the island's water table would sink under the weight of ignorant humanity, that she would always have to work to keep this love a living thing and that hurricanes would or would not come, but for this small moment she could lick the triumph on her lips. She started a slow spin in the water, felt her toes on the smooth algae, and sang out like someone who was free and wilder than wild mustangs.

The Bargain

When people say that June Ellen does not look like my sister, I explain to them that she is not my sister, she is the gift I got for my ninth birthday. June Ellen does not get offended, but will often lean over the back of my wheelchair and whisper, "You didn't think so back then."

I still have the pictures my mother took on the afternoon of that birthday. In most of them, my brother, Josh, and I are clowning around the big oak tree in the middle of the yard. June Ellen is not there yet. In one shot Josh has Spanish moss draped across his face as if it is a beard and I am holding up two fingers behind his head. But in another, I am alone in the doorway of the trailer. I am nine years old, but I look as if I already know what lies ahead, as if I can see the doctors hovering over my twenty-year-old body, as if I have already been to the funeral of a boy I think I am in love with, as if I already know that my life will not turn out the way it is supposed to.

We only lived in the trailer during the summers when

Daddy was not teaching high school biology and coaching basketball. To me it was like having a vacation house, as if we were rich folks, rather than just spending those hot months near my grandparents. My grandparents, Pawpaw and Gramma Bess, had a farm outside of Midway, Florida, a slow, quiet place with a post office, a Piggly Wiggly food store and a population of about forty other farm or laborer families. On land contiguous to Pawpaw's farm was our trailer. Back then no one called them "mobile homes."

The trailer had a road of its own off the main highway and an enormous live oak in the front yard with branches so supple you could lean back into them and lull away the summer hours like a baby in a cradle. I liked the country because I didn't have to walk Mama's dog, Bubbles, on a leash every morning. She could just run free like any country mutt. Bubbles was part terrier and part poodle. Mama had gotten Bubbles for me when Josh was born as a way of pacifying my three-year-old rage at being supplanted, but Bubbles was always Mama's dog, sitting in her lap in the evenings and licking her fingers.

We had a swimming hole on the property where Josh and I would linger in the hot afternoons, cooling ourselves in the mud while tiny fish nipped at our skin. Most days Daddy would go over to Pawpaw's farm and help out, and as long as Joshua and I never complained of being bored, we would not be required to tag along and load watermelons or pick fat black worms off Pawpaw's tomatoes. Daddy liked to collect the worms for his students to use in experiments.

"You only get to be kids for a second or two so you better live it up," Daddy told us. Mama had a special switch for when we got in her way too much or if I got a little too sassy. Josh never got the taste of that switch the way I did. Right on the back of my legs – ouch.

When Daddy would see the red switch marks, he'd say, "You were sassing your Mama again, weren't you, girl?"

"Yes, sir," I'd say, feeling respectful and slightly ashamed that I had forgotten to clean the mason jars for my mother's blackberry jam or whatever crime it was that I'd committed.

On Saturdays we would go to Pawpaw's vegetable stand on the highway and relieve him for a spell. I felt very important as I took money from the people who stopped by in their big cars, air-conditioning pouring out of the door when they opened it. They acted just like I was a grown-up, and when I told them seventy-five cents for half a bag of tomatoes, they sometimes gave me a dollar and told me to keep the change. Bubbles would sit at our feet, panting and wagging her tail, wanting nothing more than for one of the strangers to invite her into their car. That dog didn't have an ounce of loyalty.

My mama was the one who had grown up in Midway. On especially steamy afternoons she'd put on her black one-piece bathing suit and soak herself in the hole with Josh and me after lunch. Midway was the kind of place she could leave us alone while she went to help Gramma Bess out with the cooking or the curing of freshly-slaughtered pork. Everybody in Midway was friendly and would look out for kids. Everybody, that is, except for June Ellen's momma.

"That woman is the sorriest excuse for a mother I ever saw," Daddy said to Mama over dinner more than once.

"Don't be ugly in front of the children," Mama said back to him. I knew that she believed exactly what he said about June Ellen's mother. June Ellen was two years younger than me and always dirty and hiding in the woods, watching me and Josh.

"Don't look at her," I told Josh when we caught her peeking through some bushes at us. But Josh would yell at her and pretend he was a monster. I'd roll over laughing as she ran off like some kind of wild kitten. I'd only been near her once and that was at the post office where we had to go every week and I had noticed that she smelled like pee. Her momma – big as a tractor – smelled like something else and only years later would I realize that it was like fermentation.

My birthday is the first of August. And the summer I was to turn nine years old, I was just getting old enough to realize that I didn't get to have regular birthday parties because all my friends lived in town. Mama said she was sorry, but that I'd just have to settle for having family for cake and ice cream and that maybe I could have a sleep-over party in the fall when school started back up and we were back home. That year even Pawpaw and Gramma Bess could not come over for the pork chops, apple sauce, fresh pole beans, watermelon and strawberry cake with real strawberries in the icing that was my special dinner. Gramma Bess had the high blood and needed to stay off her feet.

Josh and I played outside that day.

"Put this piece of grass in your mouth, Josh," I said. He laid the long stalk across his mouth. He was still obedient to me, but especially that day because it was my birthday, and I told him he had to do everything I said on that day.

Then I yanked one end of the stalk through his mouth, shredding off the little black seeds on the end.

"What'd you do that for?" he asked, spitting out black specks.

"Look, it's clean now," I showed him.

"Those were ants," he said.

"They were not," I said, forgetting how hard I had worked to convince him that the black seeds on the end were alive, just like I'd convinced him that shells would bite you if you put your finger up to the part I said was the mouth.

He stomped away. I knew where he was going – to check on the baby owls in their burrow. There was a family of burrow owls in our field. Little gray feather balls. I followed him to our spying log and lay beside him, felt the hot grass scratching against my skin. Burrow owls are about the only owl I know of that will hunt in the daytime more than at night. Daddy told me they were "diurnal." We could watch them for hours as they foraged around for insects or stood in front of the hole where they lived, big yellow eyes like suns. Sometimes the mother owl would get angry and puff her feathers out and spread her wings, trying to scare us off.

"Look," Josh whispered. One of the owls was swooping low over the field, a mouse with a broken neck hanging from her beak. Her brown and white wings were fanned out, and I could see the shadow underneath her rippling over the grass.

After lunch Mama came out and took pictures of us. When her film ran out, she shooed us off, and Josh and I went out to the swimming hole – a big brown bowl with a weeping willow drinking from one side of it and some woods in the distance. I felt so glad to be nine years old and to know that my mother was inside the trailer kitchen spreading icing on my birthday cake. I wondered what my daddy had gotten me and if a new bicycle was even now in the back of his pickup truck. Josh was eager, too. He was always a sweet kid, and he had made me a birthday present that he could hardly stand to keep quiet about.

"Isn't it time for supper yet, Lindy?" he kept asking.

"Not yet," I said, "not yet." I was prolonging the moment as if I was blowing up a balloon, slowly adding air until the very second before it would burst.

The sky had turned absolutely white and the clouds were just a darker shade of white, little icing puffs against the sky. I lay back at the edge of the swimming hole and smelled summer like a ripe melon all around me. I knew right then that this moment would never come again and that I was growing and changing so quickly I'd never be able to keep up with myself. My eagerness and sorrow were linked together like the white and brown feathers of the owl, and I could not tell which was which.

When I could no longer stand it, I jumped up, and over my shoulder I yelled, "It's time." Off I raced with Josh huffing and puffing behind me, maddened because I had tricked him once again. Bubbles trailed behind us, yapping furiously.

When we burst into the trailer, the first thing I saw was that Mama had already set the table with birthday dinnerware and the blue tablecloth used for special occasions. The second thing I saw was June Ellen huddled on the couch with her hands clasped between her knees, her hair a black mass of tangle and her eyes nailed to the floor.

"What's she doing here?" I blurted out. I was desperate for friends in the country but not that desperate.

Mama turned from the pork chops on the stove and looked at me, smiling as if her teeth had something sticky on them and she could not close her lips.

"I thought it would be nice for you to have a little guest for your birthday party, Lindy," she said. "Now y'all go on and get dressed. We're fixing to have supper as soon as Daddy gets here."

I walked past June Ellen, both Josh and I staring at her like we'd never seen anything like her before in our lives. And to be honest, I had never seen a little girl whose face was as swollen and bruised as hers or whose arms were as thin and dirty.

"Wear a dress, Lindy," Mama called as I went into the bedroom. Then I heard her take June Ellen into the bathroom. And I heard the water running. All I could hope was that the pork chops didn't burn.

Having June Ellen there didn't exactly ruin my birthday. She didn't say a word, just gobbled the food Mama set down before her, eyes wide open as if making sure we weren't suddenly going to swat her or snatch the food back. My presents were few but nicer that year than I had remembered from years before: a white church dress made by Gramma Bess, a set of pastel crayons and charcoal pencils with a white sketch book from Mama, a handmade birdfeeder from my brother and the bicycle that I expected from Daddy.

"Maybe you could give June Ellen your old one," Mama suddenly piped up as we all stood outside looking at my new metallic purple bicycle with the white straw basket on the front. The day had begun to turn dark quickly as if the sky was clear water and the night was tea seeping over it. But even in the gloaming, I could tell by the way my father's shoulders cocked that he had given my mother a strange look.

"My old one is at home in town, Mama," I said.

"Oh, that's right," Mama said. I looked over at June Ellen, who shifted around on her feet and then stood very still like a bird hoping you haven't noticed her.

I hugged Daddy and mumbled my thanks to Mama.

We went back inside the house. Since it was my birthday, we were allowed to stay up late and watch TV. Josh and I took cushions from the couch and placed them on the floor. June Ellen did just what I did. I watched her from half-lowered lids. She didn't do anything for me to yell at her like get too close to me, but I was waiting. She made me uncomfortable with that blue bruise along the side of her face and the black rims of dirt under her fingernails.

We settled down and started watching some insipid romantic movie. Josh fell asleep and Mama sat on the couch with no cushions and tried to pretend that she wasn't crying over a stupid movie, which she always did.

The knocking on the door made us all jump, but looking at Mama I realized she wasn't all that surprised. She and Daddy said something to each other with their eyes. The knocking came again. I looked over at June Ellen. Her face was a mask, not looking at the TV, not looking at the door. She looked straight at me instead, and I shivered. Mama straightened her dress and went to the door.

I got up and edged behind her. June Ellen's skinny little father stood in the yellow outdoors light. His shoulders slowly rose up around his head as if he were a box turtle who had suddenly been discovered. He worked at the gas station and was always very nice to us in a sickening kind of way. I knew he wasn't the one who put the bruises on June Ellen's face.

"I'd be beholden to you if you'd send June Ellen home now, Miz Tatum," the scrawny little man said.

Mama looked at him and then said in her sweetest Sunday school voice, "We're just gonna keep June Ellen here, Jim. I know you and her momma won't mind."

His mouth dropped open. Mama smiled and said, "Goodnight." She shut the door in his face, and then stood there frozen at the door. I stared up at her in wonder.

We could hear that he hadn't left. He just waited there for the longest. No one moved. No one said anything. Finally I heard his feet shuffling on the ground as he walked away. Mama went back over to the couch.

"Martha, you can't just keep someone else's young

'un," Daddy said from his Lazy Boy recliner. June Ellen and I both turned toward Mama. She gave Daddy a look I had never seen before, but I registered that look in my mind in case I ever had need of it myself. Her eyes seemed to shift color, her lips compressed themselves and her nostrils flared minutely. Everything about her expression was subtle but she was so still that the movement of an eyelash seemed monumental. Daddy just shrugged. He wasn't going to fight that look.

I lay in bed that night with June Ellen sleeping beside me. I could hear the cicadas and bull frogs outside trying to out-loud each other. I'd always found those sounds soothing before but now they irritated me and I couldn't sleep. The noises subsided for a moment, and I looked out the window. Mama was throwing something in the trash. I got up and went outside. The air was warm. I felt the cooling ground under my bare feet.

"Mama?" I asked.

She turned around. I walked to the trash can and looked in.

"Lindy," she said. "I want you to promise something to me."

"What?" I asked, sullenly. I never liked promises.

"I want you to promise not to be mean to June Ellen. Do you promise?" She had her face close to mine, and I could smell the strawberries on her breath. I looked over at the trash where Mama's switch now lay.

"I promise," I said.

The next day Mama started sizing down some of my old clothes for June Ellen. The sky had clouded up overnight. Josh, June Ellen and I were inside. I was trying to draw a picture of the mama burrow owl we had seen the day before, thinking about the different shades of brown in her wings, and Josh was teaching June Ellen how to play Chinese checkers. She couldn't seem to figure it out, but Josh was patient – more than I would have been. We all stopped what we were doing when we heard a car with a bad muffler rumble into our drive. The engine choked and sputtered when it was turned off, and we all knew it had to be someone for June Ellen. I smiled but did not look up from my drawing. Mama got up and went outside.

"Quit staring out the window," I said to Josh and June Ellen, but they didn't pay attention to me, and finally I joined them. June Ellen's momma stood outside a few feet from her old Impala. Her arms were crossed and her face was crumpled-looking. My own mother stood between her and the trailer. Her long hair was twisted back behind her neck. June Ellen held her breath and couldn't take her eyes off the two of them. Her bruise had turned as purple as the storm clouds.

For a while June Ellen's momma listened to my mother and then she said something back. When she did, she was ready to spit fire, I could tell that much. She uncrossed her arms and waved them around. Then my mother, who didn't move at all but kept her hands firmly on her hips, talked to her some more. The conversation went back and forth a few times then stopped, the women just standing there. Finally, June Ellen's momma stared out toward the woods and with one hand she wiped at her face as if she was brushing off a fly. The whole time, Bubbles had been circling Mama's feet and rolling over to have her belly scratched. Then the thing I will never forget happened. Mama bent down, picked Bubbles up, kissed her, scratched her behind the ears and then offered her to June Ellen's momma. June Ellen's momma looked at the dog for a moment, and then she took her, got in her old car and left.

We had just traded our dog for someone else's kid. My

gaze met June Ellen's and it felt like I was falling down a deep well as I realized she was going to be a part of my life for a long time.

I was not mean to June Ellen, but neither was I nice to her. She came back to town with us in the fall and moved into my bedroom. I had to clear out room in the closet and half my drawers. Daddy bought another twin bed and said the room was half hers and half mine. I didn't complain. I never yelled at her, never snatched something of mine out of her hands no matter how much I wanted to, and never told her how butt-ugly I thought she really was with her pug little nose, crooked teeth and freckles. The only thing I did that could be construed as showing my true feelings was to keep Bubble's leash on a nail by my bed.

I left it there the rest of elementary school and all through junior high school. June Ellen never said a word about it. Mama treated June Ellen as if she were one of her own children. Daddy was always kind to her, but never as comfortable as he was with me and Josh. Josh, who was a year younger than June Ellen, liked her and showed her how to ride a bike, climb trees and be like other kids. But June Ellen would never really be like other kids. She didn't have any friends for one thing. After school when we got older, I'd go out to the mall or the movies with my girlfriends, and June Ellen would stay home and clean the house with Mama or watch TV.

Still, I always felt that the only one of us that June Ellen really loved was me. You could tell by the way she tried to dress like me or even say the same things I said. And she would come sit beside me not saying anything, just watching me while I sketched pictures. She was like a strange pet – an iguana or a ferret – that you keep because someone gave it to you but you don't really want.

I was biding my time until I could get out of the house and be on my own. I thought I had found my ticket during my first year of high school when I met an older boy who drove a Camaro and had a job at the supermarket. I started sneaking out of the house late at night to go to the sinkhole with him and give myself over to his smooth licking hands in the backseat of his car.

One morning at breakfast Mama said she'd come by the room and noticed I was gone, but that June Ellen explained we'd heard some raccoons outside.

"You know, Lindy, you shouldn't be going outside just to check on some old 'coons. What if someone saw you out there? What would they think?" she asked.

"They wouldn't think anything," I snapped back without even looking over at June Ellen to convey my gratitude. But that night I took the leash down from the hook by my bed.

"June Ellen, I've got something to tell you," I said. "I never did like that damn dog."

She was already in bed, her face scrubbed and her hair shiny as a doll's.

"I know," she said.

After high school I went away to the university. I stayed in state, but at least I was a good half a day away. June Ellen stayed home and got a job doing the books for a propane gas company. Mama made her take a few courses at the community college, but she said she didn't like it much whenever I asked her about it. June Ellen wasn't stupid, but she didn't like it when the teachers called on her.

I was a double major in art and biology. Daddy was pleased. It was in my biology class that I met Jim. The best-looking guy I had ever seen and he was smart enough to ace the class even if he did wear a belt buckle with his name on it. We'd been going out for six months and were thinking about moving in together. One night we were driving back to his place from a frat party. I was smoldering because he had been talking to this flippant blond who smoked black cigarettes.

I can't tell you a thing about the accident. One minute he was saying he was sorry, that he loved me; the next I was in a hospital with a cast so thick it could have been a sarcophagus, and he was dead. Everything inside me was broken.

I came out of the darkness like someone swimming out of a cave. And the first person I saw was June Ellen. She was there every day bringing wild flowers and news of my family when they couldn't be there. When it was time for me to leave, she snapped open the wheelchair and put her wiry little arm underneath me as she helped me into the seat.

"I got an apartment," she said, pushing me through those swishing hospital doors into the stark white daylight. It was difficult to imagine her doing such a thing on her own, but it was more difficult to imagine the life that was ahead of me.

No one in my family ever drank, but to tell you the truth, June Ellen and I sometimes share a bottle of wine these days with our dinner. By the second glass, I am less aware of my wheelchair, but if we ever go beyond a bottle, I begin to cry and think about the boy who died in the accident and how I thought I would marry him. I realize now that I probably would not have married him. If he had lived, we would have broken up sooner or later. But that love never had a chance to finish itself off. It's like one of my unfinished paintings, a picture only half-formed, the shapes nebulous and the colors still undecided. I gave up biology.

On weekends, June Ellen and I pack up the van with

my pictures and go to arts and crafts shows around the state. You would be surprised at how much money we make. People are especially expansive with their checkbooks when they see me in my wheelchair, paint-daubed smock and brush in my hand as I put the finishing touches on some practice piece I take with me. June Ellen, who has never been good with strangers, seems to have no problem telling people all about my painting. I guess she watched me long enough that she knows more about it than I do. Sometimes I paint something that is more than just a decoration for someone's living room wall, and those she tucks away or prices so high that she knows only someone who can appreciate them will buy them.

Just the other night we went down to the wildlife refuge. I like to have a lighthouse picture for every show. People love lighthouses though I'm a bit tired of them. I can't imagine what they represent to those people who hang pictures of them all over their houses. But lighthouses were proven money-makers, and the snapshot I'd been working from was old. I wanted a new angle, fresh light, maybe some storm clouds in the background.

"Let's have a picnic," June Ellen suggested as she folded an easel for me. She sounded just like my mother sometimes. She packed some turkey sandwiches and spooned potato salad into a Tupperware container.

"Bring a couple of slices of watermelon," I said.

She wrapped them in foil and placed it all with a bottle of chenin blanc into a paper bag. Then we drove down to the coast.

We ate first and each filled a plastic cup with wine. Then I sketched the scene in pencil as we waited for the evening light to open its eyes for us.

"Lindy, look," June Ellen said. I could smell the watermelon rinds and the wine and that deep wet earth smell of summer. I looked in the direction she was pointing, across the expanse of tall grasses, and saw a dark shape swooping low over the ground.

"A burrow owl," I said. And for a moment we were both back in Midway where we had continued to go several more summers until Gramma Bess died and Pawpaw came to live in town with us. We were both reliving those summers when she followed Josh and me around, more faithful than Bubbles ever had been. We had run into June Ellen's momma a few times, always treating that pitiful dog like she was some kind of rare AKC champion. I had been kinder to June Ellen in the country, letting her play our games or occasionally borrow the old binoculars to look at the birds we hunted down. How alive I had felt.

"June Ellen, do you ever want to have children?" I asked, thinking about the fresh unfettered joy I had felt when I was young.

"Children?" she asked as if she wasn't sure what they were. She set down her empty dixie cup. I looked over at her. She was still scrawny, but her face with its pointy chin and turned-up nose was an interesting one – a face with character we used to say. Instead of being homely, she now looked wise and almost pretty to me. She had given her whole life to me. And I didn't understand why. And at that moment, my confusion made me angry. Why wouldn't she want children? Why would she sacrifice her life? And what price did I have to pay for it?

"June Ellen, you don't have to stay with me. I'm making enough money to hire someone. Go out, get married or something." A breeze swept up from the river and brushed the hair across her face. She stared at me. I couldn't read her. I was leaning forward in that damn chair, leaning on the legs I could not feel.

She looked away, eyes squinting against the sunlight, golden on her skin. We were silent for a long, long time.

Her hand was balled into a tight fist as if she was clutching something.

"I'm not a dog. You can't trade me away," she said in a voice like black linen.

"I don't want to trade you away," I answered. "Just thought you might want more. Thought you might want children someday."

"You want children," she answered. "But for you and me, Lindy, childhood is two different things."

I looked at her for a long time, but there was no trace of the bruised and filthy little urchin she had once been. She was just June Ellen, my June Ellen. I picked up my brush and began to paint the lighthouse and the owl skimming across the grass in the distance.

Dancing For Poppa

I stood at Poppa's graveside along with my parents, cousins, aunts and uncles. Grandma leaned on my left arm as Uncle Henry threw a clod of dirt on Poppa's ivory-colored coffin. The cemetery was cooled by large oak trees shading the plots. Flower arrangements dotted the grass or lay upon the cool granite tombs. Poppa would be happy here, I hoped. But I didn't know if he would be happy with me, his only granddaughter.

"Poppa" is what I called my grandfather; he was also my friend, the one who knew my dreams. He lived in the small town of Mandarin, Florida, with Grandma in a big white house on the St John's River. I used to love to visit him and pick oranges from his trees or play on the banks of the river, catching tiny brown fiddler crabs.

When I was seven years old, Poppa came to the house and handed me a big box.

"What's in it, what's in it?" I cried.

He looked down at me with his heavy-lidded brown

eyes and said, "Open it up, Tinkerbell." And I tore the flimsy gold elastic ribbon from the box. Inside underneath the soft white paper were pink tights, a black leotard and a pair of pink ballet slippers. I looked back up at Poppa for some explanation.

"It's for your lessons," he said, "ballet lessons."

I hadn't even known that I wanted to take ballet, but when he said ballet lessons I felt that I had been asking for nothing else my whole life. I screamed with excitement and ran into my room. After I donned my new outfit, I came prancing out into the living room. My older brother, Randy, pretended to gag, Daddy said that it was very nice and Momma asked who was going to pay for these ballet lessons. Poppa said he would as I hopped around him like a little bird.

"You're going to drive into town every week to take her?" my mother asked. We lived in Jacksonville, a half hour away from his house.

"Twice a week," he said and kissed me. That night I slept in my new leotard and tights.

The next Monday Poppa took me to Ophelia Bell's School of Dance in San Marco, a quaint little shopping area with a movie theater, a community theater, a bakery, a five and dime, and several dress shops where my mother had charge accounts. The dance school was located in a big art deco building at the end of the block. We went inside.

Clasping his hand as if it were a large branch from which I dangled, I timidly looked around at the big girls who seemed so self-assured in their outfits as they waited for their own classes to begin. They laughed among themselves and stretched their sleek muscles. It was a performance in itself.

"This is Connie," Poppa said to Miss Bell, and she smiled at me. As she bent down, her cologne engulfed me. Even now whenever I smell Chantilly, I think of Miss Bell. She led me into an enormous room with wood floors and mirrors along the front wall. Standing along the other wall, about twenty little girls, all approximately my size, clung with one hand to a wooden rail, which I later learned was called the barre. I got in the back of the line.

"Just follow along," Miss Bell told me. Well, I followed along fine until suddenly everyone turned around and I was in the front of the line. I had to keep glancing over my shoulder to see what we were doing. I wanted to quit that very day. I would tell Poppa, I thought. He wouldn't make me come here again if I didn't want to. After the lesson I came out, holding my breath so that I wouldn't burst into sobs.

"You were fantastic," Poppa said. "A natural."

At the next lesson, which was on Thursday, I was smart and got a space in the middle of the barre so that I had someone to follow no matter what direction we faced. Miss Bell paced along the line with a long stick, counting the beats on the wood floorboards and sometimes using the stick to tap our tummies or our buttocks to make sure we were holding them in tight. "*Tendu*," she'd say and we all pointed our toes to the side without having the vaguest idea what *tendu* meant.

After the funeral the family returned to our house to eat baked ham, potato salad and freshly-sliced tomatoes. There was also a red velvet cake, Poppa's favorite. I helped mother serve everyone, about ten people in all. The others – friends and people who had worked with Poppa for Seaboard Coastline – had left after the service. Only the family went to the graveside and came to the house afterwards.

"Here, Grandma, let me pour your tea for you," I said and poured the hot orange-pekoe tea into a china cup.

She took it, her hand shaking, the tea cup clattering on the saucer, and I held my breath as she brought it up to her trembling lips. Miraculously, not a drop spilled.

"Why couldn't Randy make it?" she asked querulously.

"He had a final exam, Grandma, and he just couldn't get out of it," I told her for the fourth time that day.

"Pretty soon you'll be gone, too. Everyone will be gone," she said with a moan. I knew it was her way of missing Poppa, as tears slid down her cheeks.

"I'll be back for vacations, Grandma," I said, more to comfort myself than her.

"What are you going to major in, Connie?" Aunt Mary Jane asked me.

"I don't know," I said.

"Pre-law," my father said. Yuck, I thought, but smiled. He knew I didn't want to be a lawyer.

"She should do something that makes a lot of money," Aunt Lynn advised and licked some red velvet cake from her lips.

"Or marry someone who is going to make lots of money," Uncle Henry said, poking Aunt Lynn with his fork.

Grandma surprised them all by saying, "This isn't the '50s. She doesn't need to marry anybody. And she doesn't need to make a lot of money. All she needs to do is something that makes her happy. That's what her Poppa would have wanted."

"Thanks, Grandma," I said and stroked her plump little pigeon of a hand. "More tea?"

She nodded and I poured another cup for her.

"Just as long as you don't think you're going to be a ballerina," my mother said as she got up from the chair in the corner and cut herself another piece of cake. Poppa always thought I would be a ballerina. And I guess I did, too, until I was about fourteen when I realized that even though I was quite good, I wasn't good enough to be a star for a major ballet company, and I didn't want to be in a company if I was just going to be a member of the corps. I had been a star in Miss Bell's senior class, and that had spoiled me for anything but the spotlight.

For the first five years, I had been a mainstay of the back row, but I started coming in to the school and practicing by myself early in the mornings and one day Miss Bell asked me to lead the class. In our eighth-grade recital, I had my first solo. Poppa embarrassed me by standing up and clapping at the end of my performance, and he kept clapping long after it was time for the next girl to come on. He cried afterward, saying, "I am young again when I watch you up there dancing like a fairy princess. It makes me young."

A week before his death I visited him in the hospital. He wanted to know what my plans were, whether or not I was going to New York to try out for the American Ballet Theater.

"No, Poppa," I told him. "I'm going to Florida State with Cathy and my other friends from school."

"But I thought you liked performing," he said, crossing his hands. An IV tube was stuck in his arm, and he had lost at least thirty pounds, but his eyes had the same dark intensity as ever.

"I love it, but it's not enough for me. I want to do more with my life, maybe help people somehow." I couldn't explain, but I knew there was more to life for me than the stage, even if I had been good enough to be a star. He didn't say he was disappointed, but his smile seemed weak. Maybe that was just the illness.

"Come with us to your grandmother's, Connie," my mother said after I collected the plates from around the living room and took them into the kitchen.

"Would you mind if I didn't?" I leaned against the

sink. I had not been able to cry for Poppa the way everyone else had. If I could have just cried, maybe my knees wouldn't have felt as though they would sink like sandbags to the floor.

"Yes, Connie, I would mind very much." But my father overheard us from the dining room and came into the kitchen.

"Let her stay here, honey. She's been so strong for everyone else," he said and he gave my mother a long look. "They were very close," he added in a voice so soft he must have thought I couldn't hear him.

"I'll stay with her," Aunt Lynn piped in, carrying an ashtray and smoking a cigarette as she followed my father into the kitchen. Oh no, I thought. She'll chatter my head off. But fortunately my father coralled her like a shepherd's dog, herding the sheep.

"No," he said. "Then we'll have to make an extra trip to take you home. Besides, Connie will be busy cleaning up the house."

Aunt Lynn shrugged her shoulders. My mother sighed and grimaced the way she does when something is no longer important to her as my father ushered them out.

Soon the house was quiet except for the running water as I rinsed off the dishes before loading them into the dishwasher. Every dish felt heavy in my hands and I thought of the pall bearers carrying Poppa's big coffin. They kept their backs so straight as if it didn't weigh a thing, but I knew by the way their knuckles turned red that it was heavy. I scraped the pieces of leftover velvet cake into the food disposal and placed the dishes just so in the dishwasher. Then all the dishes were loaded and the dishwasher was making its churning sound and the counters were wiped and all the chairs were put back into their proper places. The house was back to normal as if

Poppa had never died, as if he would come in any moment and say, “How’s my princess?”

I sat down in the living room on the couch where earlier Aunt Lynn and Aunt Mary Jane had been discussing Poppa’s will. He had left enough to take care of Grandma and a few tokens for members of the family. He had left me a framed photograph of the Degas statue, the “Little Ballerina,” which sat on the coffee table next to the catalog from the college where I had been accepted.

I opened the catalog. There was a section for Arts and Sciences. I thumbed through the pages, perusing the courses. Some of them I would have to take: first-year composition and algebra. When I came to the page of dance classes, I stopped a moment to daydream. I imagined being on stage, felt the warmth of the lights and the tightness of the costume with its sequins and straps. I looked back at the catalog and noticed something I hadn’t seen before. Just below the list of dance courses was a section of dance therapy classes. I had never even heard of dance therapy, but it made sense. I turned to the course descriptions and found that there was even a major for dance therapy.

“Dance makes people happy,” Poppa had said one Christmas after a family dinner. “Even a little baby knows how to dance. Before she can walk or talk, she’ll start bouncing when she hears music. Look at that little one there.” Mirabella, my cousin’s daughter, was only eleven months old, and she was swaying and banging her hands to the old swing music that Poppa liked.

He was right. Dancing had always made me happy. And watching me dance had always made Poppa happy. It occurred to me that perhaps Poppa didn’t want me to cry for him. Maybe he just wanted me to be happy like Grandma had said.

I walked to my bedroom and found my toe shoes

hanging by their laces in the closet. I stuffed some fresh lambs wool in the toes, pulled on my tights and leotard and went back into the living room. We had a recording of *Swan Lake*, and I put it on. The music started, soft and sad. Instead of dancing the traditional version, I made up my own steps. My arm swung above my head and I rose up on my toe and stretched my leg out in an arabesque. My leg rose higher and straighter than it ever had before. Then I brought my foot to my knee. My body had a life of its own as I twirled. It seemed that I twirled in slow motion and that sitting on the couch, Poppa was clapping and shouting "Bravo." My torso stretched taller than ever and I could pirouette three times in one continuous spiral. Every movement was perfect. I played side one and then side two and then I started over again. I danced until with bleeding toes I landed in a lake of dreams.

The next morning my mother woke me up and said, "Hey, you slept in your ballet clothes. Might as well get up. You've only got a couple of weeks left until summer vacation is over. Better enjoy every minute of it."

She opened the window before she left. I rolled over in my bed and inhaled the last notes of my childhood. Outside a breeze danced through the leaves of a chinaberry tree, and it sounded like distant applause.

Viral Love

Jenny opened the door to the log cabin and stepped quietly into the dark living room. An aura of smoke hung about her hair, her clothes, and her skin like rancid cologne. She stumbled against the coffee table, cursed silently and then stole into the bedroom where Lyle slept half under an old brown comforter in the double bed. He was wearing his plaid robe. His wire-rimmed glasses sat on the table underneath the green desk lamp. If he were awake, he'd look like an advertisement for Cutty Sark.

She shed her sweater and jeans quickly, went into the bathroom, turned on the hot water in the shower and held her hand under the spray, waiting for the water to heat up. In a few minutes thick ribbons of steam rose into the shower. She stepped into the water and thought about the night's adventures. It had been fun to get out without him, to be with Cinny and Joanne, just girls drinking, snorting a few lines in the tiny stall of the bathroom at the bar, playing pinball. Girls night out. She could never get high with Lyle. She was supposed to be clean now.

But she was looking forward to climbing into the bed with him, pulling up the covers and curling her body next to his. As the water rushed over her skin, she closed her eyes and moved fully under the spray to get her hair wet and then reached for the bottle of Flex shampoo that she and Lyle shared. But before she reached it, Lyle was suddenly half in there with his hand around her throat pushing her against the back of the shower wall, his eyes grim and narrow.

"Who were you with tonight, Jenny?" Lyle asked in an antiseptic voice. With his other hand, he inserted a clinical, inspecting finger into her vagina.

"Shit," Jenny squawked. "No one."

He withdrew his finger and turned around as if disappointed to find her innocent. She stayed there, staring momentarily at the shower curtain that trembled where he'd dropped it. God, how stupid did he think she was? She made a mental inventory to see if she had made any mistakes in the execution of her recent activities. She just wanted a night out. What was the big deal? She could go in and scream at him self-righteously and with perfect justification. But she didn't want to fight tonight. She was high; she wanted to cuddle and kiss slowly without talk. She washed her hair, got out of the shower and wrapped a towel around herself.

He lay on the bed watching as she came in.

"Why were you taking a shower?" he asked sullenly.

"Because I stank of cigarette smoke. I know you hate that," she answered. She let the towel drop to the floor and slipped on one of his T-shirts. For a second the coke she'd done earlier had kicked back into her system, brought on by adrenalin, but now the beer was having its calming effect so that everything seemed abnormally normal in a blurry kind of way.

"I thought you'd been with someone else," he said.

"I was," she said. She sat down on the bed and dragged a comb through her wet hair. "I was with Cinny and Joanne."

The bedroom was small. The whole house was small. Six months ago she'd been intrigued with the idea of living in a log cabin – with him. She still was. She didn't want to give it up. She looked over at Lyle. His robe was open, showing his tanned belly, the indentation of his slightly furred naval and his paisley boxer shorts. He had dark brown hair, violently blue eyes and a slightly crooked nose that only heightened the effect of his beauty.

What if she had been with somebody tonight? What if he'd caught her? She lay down beside him and tried to clear her mind of guilty thoughts. It had been two weeks since she'd had beer sucking and sex with Kevin one night when Lyle was out of town. She should be free of any suspicious taint. She nuzzled next to Lyle. She had liked the feel of his finger searching her vagina. She wondered if he would do it again, now in the bed, or had his doubts about her clouded his mind and suppressed his desire? Damn her if she let his stupid jealousy ruin the night. She ran her fingernails up his thigh. Then she felt his breath inside her own mouth, his lips pressing against hers and his hand sliding along her ribcage up under the worn-soft cotton T-shirt.

The next morning she ground the coffee beans and dropped two pieces of seedy brown bread from the health food store into the toaster. Lyle had refined her, teaching her the habits of the enlightened life he'd learned from his previous girlfriend, whose name weirdly enough was Jennifer. But besides their names and that they had both slept with Lyle, there was no similarity between the two women. The other Jennifer was rather plain but she was so damn good she seemed beautiful. She taught yoga and sewed her own clothes and double-majored in education and social work. She'd been the mother that Lyle had never really had. Sane, comforting, soft-spoken, stricken when he'd decided he couldn't be with her anymore. This much Jenny figured out with her limited knowledge of psychology and from pictures, phone calls and a few letters from said-dumped girlfriend.

Jenny met Lyle in a bar, a couple of weeks after he'd broken up with Jennifer. She must have been the antidote he was looking for.

"Hi, Lyle," she'd said, glancing down at the bronze belt buckle with his name on it. "You are too fine."

He laughed, throwing his head back to cover his embarrassment and shyness, and then offered to buy her a drink. She drank her margarita and smiled coyly and tucked a matchbook with her phone number on it into his back pocket before wandering off with one of her girlfriends. He was so good-looking she almost went catatonic thinking about him.

When the phone rang the next day about 5:30, she heard a hesitant voice.

"Hi, it's Lyle," he said.

"Hi," she answered.

"You didn't write down your name," he continued. "Just your phone number."

She laughed, embarrassed. Good thing she'd been so wasted the night before. She never would have approached him. She was in her apartment alone while her roommate was out practicing basketball. She'd been glancing at the phone all afternoon, trying to ignore it but not succeeding.

"Do you want to go get some dinner?" he asked.

Jenny glanced at the plate with the remains of her spaghetti dinner sitting on the coffee table.

"Sure, I'm famished," she said.

She stuck her finger down her throat, vomited the spaghetti dinner and used nearly a bottle of emerald-green Scope before he showed up at her door.

In spite of the belt buckle, she soon learned he wasn't a genuine redneck. In fact, he was a rich man's son who had recently graduated from college and was still trying to figure out what he wanted to do with his life. He was sweet and fairly intelligent. He asked questions about who she was, what she wanted out of life, and he actually listened to the answers. She told him straight out, she'd been in a drug program recently and now she was going to college and working part-time at a film development company. She did well in science and thought she wanted to be a meteorologist someday or maybe teach earth science in a high school. She had once thought she wanted to be a doctor, but three years of addiction to cocaine and valium had pretty much wiped out that dream. She figured he should know these things. A little honesty in the beginning could buy a lot of trust in the long run. Or so she had thought.

He had been a literature major in college but now he was selling radio advertising and what he really liked doing was scuba diving. At the end of the date, he took her home and kissed her sweet as bubblegum on the lips. She liked the way he kissed. But more than that, she wanted him to like her, this good, clean boy-man. She wanted to know that someone like him could like her. She needed proof. A month later she got it when he asked her to move in with him.

Lyle drank his coffee and ate a piece of the buttered toast.

"You want to go out to dinner tonight?" he asked.

"Definitely," she said. Jenny loved the morning after a disagreement. He might even bring home flowers. And she would be good. She wouldn't go out with her girlfriends and do septum damage. She wouldn't call Kevin today and pour out her heart. She'd clean the house instead, go to her classes and then get dressed up in something sexy to go out to a nice dinner. On the way home they might stop by the lake, and have sex teenage-style using hands and mouths, furtively pushing clothes half off, staining themselves with desire.

Lyle was almost at the front door when the phone began to ring. He smiled smugly at Jenny.

"I'm not here," he said and walked out.

Jenny picked up the phone.

"Hello."

"Jenny! It's me. Where's Lyle? Has he gone to work yet? Guess what I got yesterday. Did you know I had a tooth pulled? Where's Lyle, Jenny?"

"Hello, Meredith," Jenny said. She glanced at the clock. It was 8:30. She put the phone down and started putting away dishes. She could hear Meredith's voice, loud and raspy and incoherent. After ten minutes, she picked up the phone.

"I like you better than that other Jennifer. I know Lyle's dad liked her better, but what does he know about what's best for Lyle. He doesn't know anything. He wants to put me back in the hospital, did you know that, Jenny?"

"I have to go now, Meredith," Jenny said. "Talk to you later."

She hung up the phone. She couldn't help pitying Lyle with a mother like that. Was she ever normal, she'd asked him once. He said he couldn't remember, but he did know that once upon a time she'd been a real beauty. Now, she weighed about 250 pounds and her hair was filthy, always matted. Not that Jenny's mother would win any parent of the year awards, but at least she didn't call thirty-seven times a day. In fact, she never called.

Jenny finished getting ready for school, gathered up her books and was headed outside to her old Chevrolet when a figure shambling up the driveway caught her attention. She stopped and stared.

"What are you doing here?" she asked.

"I got Todd to drop me off down the street on his way to work," Kevin said. He wore a pair of loud Bermuda shorts and a Budweiser T-shirt. "I figured the man of the house was already gone."

Jenny couldn't help smiling at him, her partner in crimes of infidelity.

"Well, come on. We can stop at the Krystal and get some coffee before class," she said.

They got into her car and drove out of the neighborhood where the little rented log cabin was oddly situated among affluent family homes with mini-vans in most of the driveways. Kevin was not particularly good-looking except that his eyes were maple syrup-dark and penetrating through a forest of lashes. He wasn't in the same league as Lyle, who had a long list of ladies in waiting – the cashier at the supermarket who blushed and stammered and nearly cried when he smiled at her, the waitresses at restaurants they frequented, the girl at the local Laundromat who threw a fit when she first found Jenny's black bikini underwear in his weekly drop off, the secretary at the radio station where he worked. Women she barely knew would comment on her boyfriend's looks and stare at her as if wondering how she'd landed him. Not that she wasn't pretty, she was – in a sleepy-eyed decadent way, but she didn't stop traffic the way he did.

Kevin reached over and put a hand on her shoulder. No, Kevin wasn't a glamor boy. But he was funny and warm and smart in the most natural unassuming way, and he loved her though he hated himself for it, and if she could be honest about it she'd admit that she loved him more than she'd ever love Lyle. Yet Lyle was the lord of the manor, and Kevin was the secret passion in some weird transplanted-to-the-twenty-first-century version of courtly love.

"So does Prince Charming suspect anything?" Kevin asked as they sat down at a red Formica table in the Krystal across from campus, or "Kampus," as Kevin liked to spell it.

"Sure he does, but he can't figure it out. Last night he started choking me in the shower," Jenny said, wide-eyed and almost laughing.

Kevin closed his eyes, sucked in his breath and opened them again.

"This is the second time he's pulled this shit, Jenny. Why do you stay with him?" Kevin had asked this question before. And she hadn't known what to say then either. Was it the fact that Lyle was a working guy who could afford a cute little house and take her out to nice dinners? Or his heartbreaking looks?

"It's just the way I am, Kev," she said. "I don't stop reading a book until I get to the last page even if I hate it. I don't leave a movie until the last credit rolls, you know where the writing is tiny and they're telling you what kind of camera they used. I can't leave until it's over. And it's just not over."

Kevin shook his head.

"Remember that humanities class I took last semester?" he asked. Jenny stared at his reflection in the window rather than look at him.

"Oh yeah, the famous Dr Sue," she said. She didn't know what half the campus saw in her. The woman had to be over forty, but she had a following, especially among the guys.

"She once said that people who are unconscious have no choice in their behaviors. Some Indian guru told her that ninety-nine per cent of us are asleep. If we were awake, we would have a choice," Kevin said.

Jenny sighed and leaned back against the cold plastic seat. A cup of coffee steamed in front of her.

"He doesn't hurt me," she said, thinking back to the time Lyle had slapped her on the forehead when he had suspected her of holding hands with a friend of his whom she couldn't stand. "It doesn't even hurt. That's what amazes me."

"Do you want it to hurt?" Kevin asked.

Jenny slitted her eyes, gave him a what-do-you-think? sneer and gathered her book bag from the floor.

Outside the building to her class, Kevin stopped her.

"So does he have any more high school reunions coming up?" Kevin asked, his eyes trying to bore into hers.

"No, Kevin, I can't . . ." She started to say she couldn't sleep with him again, but she felt dizzy and glanced around instead. A bush beside the red brick building had erupted into pink blooms two days earlier. Jenny laughed and felt her equilibrium return. "No, he doesn't. But maybe I'll have one, and I'll have to go out of town for the weekend."

Then she leaned forward and placed her cheek against Kevin's chest.

She stopped at the black mailbox before driving down the pine-needle covered driveway: an electric bill, an envelope with Jenny's mother's return address written in black ink and a square envelope with Lyle's name and address written in curling pink letters.

She knew that the envelope from her mother contained a check. She hadn't spoken to her mother since she was seventeen years old, but ever since she finished the drug program and started going to college, her mother sent her a check every month. No letter. Just a check.

Jenny went inside the house, sat down on the toilet to pee and stared at the card for Lyle. The return address was Lyle's hometown in South Carolina. She tried to see through the envelope, but she couldn't. She finished her business in the bathroom, got up and took the letter into the kitchen. She could steam it open. That's what they always did in the movies, but then she decided no, she'd open it, read it and throw it away, pretend it never arrived. She stuck her thumbnail in the crease of the envelope and sliced it open.

Jenny stared at the card. Oh, my. A sunset. How pretty. And inside big curlicue letters. *It was so wonderful to see you again. An unforgettable night. Really enjoyed talking to you. Hope you'll come back for a visit.* Good grief. Longing in every syllable. Women could be so pathetic. And she'd been the same way, knock-kneed by this guy's looks. It was signed: *Thinking of you, Allison.* She must have agonized for hours over how to sign the damn thing.

Jenny ripped the card into shreds and jammed it into the garbage. Then she pulled up the green plastic bag, tied it around the top and took it outside. She went back inside, took a shower, sprayed herself with Opium and dressed in her ivory outfit: tight short skirt, plunge neckline top, little beige heels.

"Mmm, you look delicious," Lyle said and kissed her. She didn't kiss him back.

"What's wrong?" he asked.

She gazed at him solemnly as if she were his teacher

and she'd found his cheat sheet. She said, "Lyle, Allison called today."

"Allison?"

"From South Carolina. She told me everything."

"Oh." His lips pursed guiltily. He was so easy.

"She said you kissed her, and that she's in love with you."

Lyle stared down at the rug and then out the window. "Yes, I kissed her. I mean, what the hell. I didn't plan on ever seeing her again."

"How am I supposed to trust you?" Jenny asked.

"Trust me?" Lyle looked at her. There was a long, uncomfortable pause, but Jenny didn't let her eyes leave his. Then he spoke, "Jenny, why doesn't your mother ever write you or call you? Why does she just send you a check once a month?" Damn him. He always brought up her relationship with her mother when he didn't want to talk about something. He thought he was some kind of amateur shrink since his own mother was bats. And Jenny always deftly changed the subject back in his direction, but now she wondered, why not tell him? Tell him the truth. Even though she was just as guilty, this crap with Allison suddenly hurt her like a hot coal in her belly.

"She caught me in bed with her third husband," Jenny said, settling down into one of the kitchen chairs. Lyle sat down in the other chair and faced her.

"Did he force you?" Lyle asked.

"No," Jenny said. "I wanted to be with him. Then she came in and found us. She threw me the hell out, but she kept him." She stared hard at Lyle. This was the poisonous secret she'd never told anyone, not even the counselors at the drug program. And how could you explain it to anyone? How could anyone understand that you couldn't say no to the only affection that had ever been offered? She would have done anything for that touch that felt almost like love.

"Jesus, Jenny," Lyle said. "What the hell were you thinking?"

Jenny shook her head. This wasn't about just her.

"Don't get coy, Lyle. Tell me this. Why did you break up with Jennifer? Good, kind, button-sewing Jennifer. Not only does she sport a halo, she adored you. She'd stand by you and never lie to you. But you left her. Know why? Because you can't stand to be loved," Jenny hissed. "And this Allison is probably from the same mold. All sweet and clean who dots her i's with little hearts and giggles when she drinks. I bet you didn't even fuck her, you fool."

Lyle's hand struck her face so swiftly that even he seemed not to know where it came from. Her cheek stung. Jenny felt as if she'd plunged into an icy pond and now she was shooting back out of the water, rising, the chair falling back away from her. She shivered involuntarily, and in his confusion Lyle also stood up quickly, walked to the stereo and with a snap of his wrist turned on the radio. "Roxanne" blared out of the speakers. He switched the radio off, turned and stared at her with wet wide-open eyes. His cheeks, those tanned sheets of skin over marble cheekbones, were pink as if he'd been the one slapped. A warm stiletto blade of pleasure shot straight up through her. Her chest tightened as she suppressed a laugh. Focus, she advised herself silently. She understood in that moment that battle tasted like red wine, and she was alive, engaged in the conflict. All the sweet ladies waiting for this man would have to keep waiting. She wasn't done with him, and she knew in the hard shell of her heart he wasn't done with her. He needed someone to hurt. And so did she.

"I'm still hungry," she said. She wanted an expensive meal tonight.

He placed his hands on his hips, stared down at the shag rug and sighed.

"I need a shower," he said finally.

"I'll be outside."

She walked quickly past him and stood outside on the concrete patio. A pale lavender sky leaned over the pine trees. She had counted the pine trees when she first moved in. There were fourteen in this yard, and the little cabin was hidden behind them off the street.

As she stared up at the gnarled limbs of the trees, Jenny wondered if she was wrong in the analogy she had given Kevin. Perhaps, this thing she had with Lyle was not like a book or a movie. Instead it was a disease that hadn't yet run its course. When it had, they would both walk away feeling better. Someday she might actually feel worthy of someone like Kevin, and maybe Lyle could be with a Jennifer or an Allison.

Lyle stepped out of the house and stood on the steps. He wore a blue oxford shirt and khaki pants.

"Let's go," he said and jingled the car keys impatiently.

She followed him to the car, but it was slow going because her heels kept sinking into the black dirt.

Some Place to Live

A few days after he saves his mother's life, Joey and his sister, Aileen, come home from summer day camp to find all their clothes packed into the trunk of the rusted Bonneville. His mother says they are moving and tells them to take whatever toys they want and give the rest away.

Early the next morning, while there is still dew on the thick grass, they leave. They drive by Ballard Elementary. It is made of yellow brick with a peaked roof over the doorway. Joey waves goodbye to it. He sticks his head out of the window and looks one last time at the playground covered with pine needles that make a crispy sound when you walk on them. He sees all the play things made out of old tires. He sees the benches which are worn slabs of wood nailed to the pine trees. That is where he ate lunch every day during school with Mick and Sammy – in the shade there. He feels the air come hard from his chest. That is how he knows that he wants to cry, but he holds the tears in as if holding his breath, as if going under water.

Will we ever come back? he asks his mother.

Never, ever, ever, she says.

What about Meemaw? Aileen asks.

Your grandmother can come visit us in Florida.

Aileen doesn't mind leaving. She only went to Ballard Elementary one year, and she had the one mean teacher in the whole school. Besides, nothing bothers Aileen. Joey remembers the night when he saved his mother's life. He heard her screaming in his sleep, and finally the screams tore him away from his dreams. Fire, he thought. His feet hit the wood floor, and he ran over to Aileen's bed across the room. Get up, he screamed, shaking her. Fire.

Aileen's eyes opened and she tumbled out of the bed. They ran out of the room toward their mother's screams. But when they got into the living room, the house was not on fire. Their mother kept screaming, get out, get out, and there was a man, a strange man with his back turned to them, pulling their mother, his arm wrapped around her neck. Joey remembers the way she waved her hand at him to go. So he did, pulling Aileen out the front door as the strange man pulled his mother through the kitchen toward the back door.

Joey and Aileen ran next door to the Watsons'. He still remembers every detail, the sandspurs stuck in his foot, how Mrs Watson's face looked wrinkled and pink, and how Mr Watson stood in his boxer shorts and ripped open drawers, looking for bullets. Mrs Watson called the police, and Mr Watson had a gun, but Aileen didn't understand. Maybe he's a good guy, she said.

No, no, he's a bad guy, honey, he has your mother, Mrs Watson said.

They drive into Jacksonville later in the morning,

passing through a sulfur stench that his mother says comes from a papermill. His mother went to college here before Joey was born, and this is where she wants to live. Joey says maybe she could live in Jacksonville and he could stay at home in Brunswick. Then she could come visit. Joey's mother doesn't answer.

She parks in front of a 7–11 store and gets out to buy a paper from the machine. Joey has never seen such a fancy small store. In the car, Aileen has her baby doll. She has undressed it and laid it on the back seat between them. Joey thinks back to that night again, running through the house ahead of Mr Watson, the quiet emptiness of the living room, the book face down on the floor, the dishes still piled in the kitchen sink and the back door broken inwards, splintered at the hinges, open the wrong way. And the sounds from outside, rustling and panting like wild dogs and his mother crying. He ran into the black night, followed by Mr Watson. Then the sound of the gunshot careened in his head. A moment later he saw his mother in the grass, and a dark figure lunged into the woods behind the house, the woods where Joey's fort was.

He takes Aileen's blanket and covers the doll. Aileen reaches over and grabs his hand. They wrestle silently while their mother searches the pages of the paper for some place to live. Then she gets out and goes to the pay phone. A little later she comes back. No kids allowed, she says. The next one is too expensive, and the one after that is in a bad neighborhood. By late afternoon, they have gone and looked at about five places and none of them is any good.

Why don't we get another house? Joey asks.

Too expensive, his mother answers. And not safe.

The house that Joey likes best is the one where Mick and Sammy live just across the street from their old house in Brunswick. He likes the front screen door. It is black metal and has a big black metal bird on the bottom half. Their father has put two deer statues in the front yard. His own yard always needed mowing, even when his dad still lived there. Joey tried to mow it himself but it was hard to run the ancient lawnmower that did not even have a motor. Although Mick and Sammy's yard always looks nice, Joey is glad that he doesn't have a father anymore because Mick and Sammy's dad beats them with a belt when they do something wrong. Joey's mother has never hit him. Sammy had told him that when they heard Joey's mother screaming, they hadn't called the police because they thought it was just Joey's dad come back. And Joey said, Momma never screamed when Daddy hit her.

His mother is looking for an address as they drive through an area she calls Riverside. All the houses they pass are two-story and mostly red-brick. There is no one in any of the yards. It's an upstairs apartment, she says, in one of these houses. They pull into the driveway of another two-story red-brick house with a large covered porch. A lady who is older than Meemaw and skinny like she is made of sticks stands on the steps and grimaces at them, and Joey wonders if she is mad about something. But when they get out, her face wrinkles up into a smile.

Children, she says, isn't that nice? She reaches for Joey's cheek and pulls it. I hope they won't be too noisy. There's a lot of elderly in this neighborhood. She points to the big white brick house next door. The man who lives there is ninety years old, the lady says. Massive old oak trees dot the yard, and the Spanish moss hanging from their branches looks like old beards. Joey wishes he were back home, playing fort with Mick and Sammy.

I bet he doesn't even own a gun, Joey says, and his mother gives him a sharp look.

The old lady walks up three concrete steps along the

side of the house. She opens a door and steps in, followed by Joey and Aileen. Joey's mother stops to examine the door. There is a glass window at the top but it's too small for someone to crawl through. Joey's mother knocks on the door. Solid, she says. Joey and Aileen watch her from the landing inside. You have the whole second floor here, the landlady is saying, but their mother isn't listening. She shuts the door, she opens it, and she shuts it again. She fastens the thick chain lock and pats it.

Is this the only door? she calls up to the landlady who is perched at the top of the stairs.

Yes, the lady answers.

We'll take it, their mother says.

Joey and Aileen have not met any other kids in the neighborhood. They don't think there are any. They didn't have room for his bicycle in the car so it stayed in Brunswick at Meemaw's. Joey and Aileen play together in the backyard every day. They climb a wall at the back and climb onto the roofs of garages on either end of the wall, and from there they can climb onto other roofs. Aileen is a good jumper, and Joey is glad she can keep up with him. It would have made him mad in Brunswick if she had tagged along with him and Mick and Sammy. But now he invents spy games and lets her be a soldier or a spy or whatever the game calls for. You are good at dying, he tells her.

One day he pretends he has Mr Watson's gun and he crouches low on the flat roof behind a brick ledge, smelling the hot tar. Aileen is on the other roof. She steps down on the wall to come over to him, and Joey aims the gun at her and shoots. Aileen grabs her chest and staggers back, her mouth open in an oh, and her eyes squeezed shut. The wall is only a few inches wide and Joey yells at her to stop but her foot has already slipped and she tumbles off, screaming loudly before she hits the ground. Joey leaps off the roof and onto the wall, then drops six feet to the ground.

Lying on the ground in the dirt, Aileen gasps for breath. Then in an instant she is up and crying, running toward the house. Joey runs after her. Aileen flies up the stairs, crying and screaming the whole way. Their mother sits on her bed, watching a blue jay at the feeder outside her window. When she sees Aileen, her gray eyes widen. She gets up quickly, and Joey thinks she is going to hold Aileen and comfort her, but instead she ignores Aileen and yanks Joey by the arm, yelling at him, what did you do to her?

He can't answer, only stares. His mother is tall with blond hair that hangs past her shoulders. He has no idea who she is. She spins him around and hits him on the back of the legs with her hand, sharp stinging slaps. Aileen cries harder.

Now go, their mother says and slams the bedroom behind them. Joey spends the rest of the day cradled in the branches of the mimosa tree by the driveway, shredding the soft feathery pink flowers, wondering if they are poisonous or if you could live off flowers and leaves and never have to go home.

That night their mother makes hamburgers for dinner in the narrow kitchen at the back of the apartment. Her hair has grown shaggy. Joey sees gray strands in it. She has freckles on her arms. He has not sat on her lap since that night when the police questioned them in the living room and the policeman said to her, you know, ma'am, this wouldn't have happened if there had been a man in the house. And she had said, there is a man in the house, he's the one who got help. Then everyone said how brave he was, and Joey felt like someone on a television show.

Later that night he hears a ghost. He gets out of bed and goes to his mother's room. She is lying on the double bed, moaning in her sleep. Approaching on tiptoes, he shakes her. Her eyes flutter open, and she pulls him into her arms. I'm sorry, she says. He sleeps the rest of the night with his arm draped over her, and she doesn't moan anymore.

A few days later, she says it is time to see where they will go to school. The only school Joey can imagine is Ballard Elementary with the tall windows on either side of the front door or the Brunswick Academy where his mother taught high school.

He has GI Joe in the back seat, mounting an assault on the Russian spies. The spies are under the front seat and GI Joe has to be careful. GI Joe parachutes off the back of Aileen's head. Aileen gasps and Joey looks up. The car is idling in front of a two-story tan building. It looks bigger than any place he ever saw in Brunswick. He jams GI Joe headfirst into the floorboard.

It's gross, Aileen says. There's no grass.

What's that green slime around the bottom? Joey asks.

Their mother doesn't answer. She is hunched over, looking out Aileen's window.

We can't go to school here, Joey says. It's some kind of prison.

Where is the playground? Aileen asks.

And the jungle gym?

Their mother touches the backs of her fingers to her lips and finally says, I think they take the kids to a park for play period. Yes, that's what the lady said. We'll find the park.

The park is better. The toys are not made out of tires, but there are swings, a slide, a basketball court and colorful things to climb on, things that look like dinosaurs and Swiss cheese. Aileen runs over to the slide, calling to Joey.

Throw some dirt on the slide, she says, laughing.

Joey grabs a handful of dirt and then sees the kid under the slide. As Aileen runs around to the ladder, the kid sticks his foot out and trips her. She stumbles and lands face first in the dirt. Joey throws down the dirt and runs over to the kid, a big kid with a buzz haircut. Snarling, Joey leaps up, fists whirling. But the kid is bigger and pushes him back. Joey looks around, finds a fallen branch, picks it up and swings at the boy. He hears howling, and suddenly a piece of yellow cloth comes between them. His mother has him by the arm and drags him back to the car. Aileen hurries behind them, wiping the dirt from her clothes.

We're not going to that school, Joey says that night. We can stay here and learn at home.

OK, his mother answers. I'm too tired to fight any more. Maybe I won't go to school either. Maybe I won't teach, and then we won't have any money. We'll go on welfare.

Meemaw says that's a bad word, Aileen says. Joey doesn't know what welfare is, but he knows a prison when he sees one.

Momma, Joey asks, did they ever catch that man? Maybe he's in jail, maybe we could go back home.

She pours some milk into a glass and hands it to him.

No, they didn't catch him. This is our home. You have to accept that, Joey. We're not going back to Brunswick ever, she says.

After dinner and their baths, Joey and Aileen play marble kingdom on the oval rug in the living room. A breeze blows through the windows. Outside a round summer moon glows orange. Joey can see it over the branches of the pecan tree. Aileen says the purple marble is the princess. Joey builds the boundaries of a castle for the princess out of pencils.

Here is the living room, he says. He makes an opening for the front door.

Aileen pulls out the green shooter marble and says it is the dragon. She is wearing a pink Barbie nightgown, and she rests her round cheek on one hand.

The dragon wants to get in the castle, Joey says, pushing the green shooter through the pencils.

Wait, Aileen says. Why doesn't the princess run away?

She can't, Joey says. He doesn't know how he knows this, but he knows he is right.

Why not? Aileen asks.

The dragon will eat her children if she does, he says, and now he remembers how the door was already standing open when they came out of their bedroom. She would have had time to run. She heard the back door cave in. She had plenty of time to get out, but she had kept screaming, get out, get out, and her eyes were waiting, waiting for them before she stopped fighting, before she stopped screaming. The breeze coming in the window sends goosebumps on his arms. His head is light. Aileen's voice faraway. Then everything around him sharpens into focus and becomes solid and real once again, the many colors of the rug, the smell of summer, the hum of the attic fan drawing in air. His sister picks at a scab on her knee. His mother stands in the doorway watching them, her hand resting on the back of her neck.

Joey picks up the purple marble and bashes the dragon. The princess kills the dragon, he says.

The next day their mother tells them to get in the car because she has a surprise for them. If they don't like the surprise, then she won't make them go to the ugly school. Get in the front seat, both of you, she says.

They share the bench seat of the hot car, and Joey rolls down the window. Aileen plays with the knobs of the radio that doesn't work. An old caterpillar nest hangs white and wispy in the forked limbs of the mimosa tree.

What if we like it, but not very much? Aileen asks. What if we like it at first but then later don't?

Shut up, Aileen, Joey says. A deal is a deal.

He imagines sawing down trees with his hand as they pull out of the driveway and drive along Riverside Avenue and across the bridge to the other side of town. They pass a shopping center with a Winn Dixie grocery store and a drugstore. Then their mother turns into a neighborhood. Joey wonders if they are going to someone's house. The streets of this neighborhood are smooth and black. They speed past fancy houses with large, sloping yards and new cars in driveways. Their mother grips the steering wheel and stares ahead grimly. Suddenly, she guns the motor and bites her bottom lip. Aileen grabs Joey's hand. Ahead, a small bridge with white stone railings rises in the road. The car surges up the incline, the engine roars, and then the car soars over the crest. They float above a dip in the road for a breathless moment. Joey imagines they are all riding on a rocket ship to outer space. And then they are on the road again.

That was Thrill Hill, their mother says, laughing. Aileen falls against him and muffles her laughter into his shirt. Their mother pulls to a stop sign, and turns to look at Joey. Her gray eyes shine as her lips turn up in a smile.

Want to do it again? she asks.

Joey nods and says, yes, Momma, that was good.

The End

When my husband, Stanley, gets out of the shower, he shakes himself like a St Bernard fresh out of the pond, drenching everything in the bathroom – the towels, the sink, the three varieties of toothpaste, the two hairbrushes, the toilet seat, the walls, the door, the floor and the ceiling. Every time I look in the bathroom after he's had a shower, I stare in horror. The layer of black dog hairs on the floor doesn't help.

Stanley loves to bring me bad news.

"This blanket is teaming with fleas," he says when I lie down next to him on the king-size bed in the room where we sleep. "Ten of them jumped on me as soon as I lay down on it, and four of them got away."

"My hero," I respond.

"Did you know," he asks, "that the world's largest flea was discovered in 1913? It was a third of an inch long."

I could live without knowing that fact.

No fleas jump on me, but then again I have this bizarre

acidic skin flavor that causes my arms and hands to turn black if I touch aluminum. We discovered this in a canoe with aluminum paddles one time. Mosquitoes have little interest in me if there is anything else around with blood.

Our whole house needs to be condemned. An enormous swamp has sprung on the rug in our hallway. Apparently if water gets on the floor in the bathroom, it seeps through the caulking around the tub and then collects in the hall. In one of the bathrooms, the shower leaks profusely; the toilet in the other bathroom needs to be jiggled after every flush. My daughter woke me at three this morning to announce that she had "jiggled the potty." I read in *USA Today* recently that the most common phrase ever heard in a redneck household is "Will someone go jiggle the toilet?" The landlord says he'll come by in a week or two. In the meantime, he wants to know would I mind using *my* towels to dry up the swamp in the hallway so his rug doesn't rot?

The only room I can stay in for any length of time is my office. My office is much like my mind. It is full of information. The only problem is that I can never find the information when I need it. For instance, the insurance papers. I have been trying to get health insurance for Stanley and me and our little girl since the beginning of the summer. This has not been easy. Eight years ago, Stanley had hypertension for about three months. In a rather naive move, he mentioned this to the insurance person. Then the insurance company wanted proof his blood pressure was back to normal. Since Stanley has a pilot's license and had gotten a recent flight physical, we thought it would be no problem. We'd just have them send over those records. The doctor refused to send the information. It took us until August to get one lousy piece of paper. Then the insurance company said that wasn't enough and turned us down anyway. Now they've sent me some new papers to get filled out by another doctor. But I've lost them.

We are driving to Eckerd's in the rain to get some prints I had dropped off a week ago. We pass a schoolyard teaming with young boys, hopping around in the rain like fleas on a green blanket. Their parents watch them from umbrellad lawn-chairs. And the Little League coaches pace across the wet grass.

"They're making them play in the rain," I tell Stanley.

"What if we'd had a boy?" Stanley suddenly wonders. "And what if he was interested in sports? We'd have to take him to Little League practise every day, have to pretend like we cared. Have to stand in the rain for all his games."

"And what a terrible father you'd be," I say. "He'd tell people how you never played catch with him like that guy across the street does with his kids."

"It would be really bad," Stanley says. "Really bad."

We buy our daughter an extra doll when we pick up the prints at Eckerd's. I also pick up some flea spray for Poochus Pilate.

My life should also be condemned. Pellets of dogfood roll around the back seat of my car, which smells from all the rain. The backs of my bottom teeth are green. I cannot see the backs of my top teeth. I've been calling every day to get a cheap cleaning, but the receptionist is never there.

Stanley always props the front screen door of our house wide open. I think this looks trashy and is way too much of an indication of the way our house looks inside, which is indescribable disorder. But Stanley thinks it is too much trouble to open the front door and a screen door.

Though I say it is indescribable, I am going to try to help you picture the inside of my house. When you first come in, you will smell the rotting hallway carpet. Just beyond the carpet is a pile of clothes and towels that Stanley has tossed there in lieu of using the clothes hamper. (His office resembles a hamster cage, and so I will not take you in there.) In one corner of the entrance way is a soiled towel which I used to try to dry the swamp in the hallway. In the living room, Stanley has his computer on a small table. He has wired one of those long multiple outlets plugs to the leg of this table. On the end table next to the couch his printer sits along with several thousand documents of one sort or another. On the floor, you will see wads of paper. Stanley loves to wad up trash. Then he leaves it on the floor. I do not pick it up. You will also see two belts lying across the other couch, a pair of pants draped over a chair, possibly a pair of underpants on the floor somewhere and a three-hole punch on the arm of the couch. Our daughter has interspersed her puzzles, books and blankets among Stanley's things, but at least she usually picks up after herself. Several boxes full of electronic parts and plastic bubblewrap are stacked around the wall. We all enjoy walking on the bubblewrap and hearing it pop. I'm thinking of placing it in front of all the doorways for a burglar alarm. Poochus Pilate doesn't like it, however.

Stanley works in televised sports, and so he travels a lot. When he goes out of town, I simply shovel everything into his hamster cage, vacuum the living room floor and sigh with contentment as I feel myself edging up toward the lower middle class.

There are so many things I hate about living in the contemporary world that I don't know where to begin. I'm sitting right now in a coffee shop near my daughter's pre-school. I thought I'd come in and get a little writing done. Writing in restaurants like dislocated Parisians is what my friends do. They say it helps alleviate the isolation. But everywhere I go, my eardrums are assaulted by noise.

I see a woman, a young woman who already looks middle-aged, sitting at a table with an older man. She wears purple stretch shorts and a purple flowered shirt, the kind someone's grandmother might wear. She is plump and pale and morose-looking. I wish I knew why she was so sad. Then I could get my mind off this obnoxious music rattling around my brain pan. Why does no one else seem to notice it? And why is it everywhere I go? Loud, loud music. I never have conversations with anyone anymore except through e-mail because it is impossible with all the noise. I was at the doctor's office not long ago and thought I'd get some reading done during the usual five-hour wait. But the doctor's office insisted that I watch soap operas instead. At the McDonald's down the street I tried to meet with a client about some copy she wanted written for her bank. But Oprah was on the big screen. We couldn't hear each other. It was like those dreams where you try to scream and nothing comes out. There's another place in town, a quaintly-decorated place with baskets hanging from the ceiling, but in the middle of the room is this large black monolith with television screens facing in all directions. Stanley says it looks like *2001*. He expects people to pick up their knives and forks and start dancing around the monolith. I'm reminded more of Orwell, who had the right idea but had it backwards. We don't need to be watched all the time to stay out of trouble because we're all hypnotized by what we're watching.

I am at the threshold of my fortieth year on this planet. I know this by the fact that men no longer look at me. Actually, that's not such a bad thing. What is bad is that not only do they not look, they also do not see. This can be annoying when you are expecting the person selling you a bagel to at least make eye contact. Even the highway workers no longer see me. That really burns me. I always make a point to admire their muscled-up bods as they stand on the side of the road, flagging me by with one of their little orange banners that they handle so efficiently. Sometimes my girlfriends and I will get in my Mustang and drive by a construction site, hang our heads out the window and whistle and holler and hoot. I think that construction workers are the male equivalent of Hooter's Girls.

Fifteen minutes after we met, Stanley and I ran out of things to talk about. This has been one of the strengths of our marriage. We are not surprised ten years later to find ourselves lying next to each other in the king-sized bed with nothing to say. Instead of invading the privacy of each other's mind, we roll together and begin the slow process of arousing one another so that the marriage remains a steady center in our lives. We cling to each other like Dorothy and Toto as the icons of our world swirl around us, cackling in glee.

"Beyond that door, there's danger," Stanley always says. He should know. He says he might get a row of airline seats to sleep on instead of sleeping in the bed. That way he'll never know how miserable he really is when he travels.

Sometimes at night after our daughter has gone to bed, I will read to Stanley. He's developed a fondness for the sixteenth-century curate and writer Rabelais. In his four-volume history of giants entitled *The Life of Gargantua and Pantagruel*, Rabelais describes Gargantua this way:

> He wallowed in the mud, smudged his nose, dirtied his face, ran his shoes over at the heels, frequently caught

> flies with his mouth, and liked to chase the butterflies of his father's realm. He pissed over his shoes, shit in his shirt, wiped his nose on his sleeve, dropped snot in his soup, and paddled around everywhere. He drank out of his slipper and ordinarily scratched his belly with a basket. He sharpened his teeth on a top, washed his hands in his porridge and combed his hair with a goblet. He would set his butt on the ground between two chairs and cover his head with a wet sack. He drank when he ate his soup, ate his cake without bread, bit when he laughed and laughed when he bit, often spit in the basin, farted from fatness, pissed against the sun and hid himself in the water from fear of the rain.

Stanley loves that shit.

Some people have asked me why I married Stanley. My only answer is that Stanley is the closest I could ever get to a normal man. Every other guy I ever liked was either a drug addict, an alcoholic, married, a convicted felon, broke or a psycho. Stanley is not really normal. He doesn't like people very much. And unlike other guys, he hates sports.

"If only the NFL would go on strike," Stanley says. "Then it would be a good year."

A friend of mine works for one of those mega-hotels in Orlando. Recently, MCI, my very own long-distance company, had their convention there. They gave their top salesman or woman a brand new Lotus. The car, not the flower. Someone else got a boat.

"You should have seen the food and wine those people sucked down," my friend said. "Tables and tables full. All of it free. Women started dancing on the tables. The men were rooting under the tables like wild hogs."

The day after my friend tells me this, I get a "reminder" from MCI for a bill that had been postmarked five days earlier. I'm thinking, they can't even give me five fucking days to pay my bill? I guess the payments on that Lotus are due. I call up MCI to cancel my service. I tell the guy on the other end of the line that his company just gave a salesperson a brand new Lotus.

"I'm making seven dollars an hour," the guy says. "They say they can't afford to give us any more than that."

"You're getting screwed," I tell him.

The worst invention, the very worst invention, is the airport automatic-flushing toilet. Am I the only person in the world who thinks this must be the most egregious waste of water imaginable? The second you walk in the stall the damn thing starts flushing, *whoooooshshshshshshsh-shsh*. You sit down and it flushes again, *whooosh-shshshshshshsh*, making sure your privates get a nice cold douche in the process. You finish, but before you rise, it flushes again, *whoooooshshshshshshshsh*. It probably flushes three or four more times before you lurch out, your jeans wrapped around your knees, and fall onto the tile floor, begging, no more please, no more.

No, the worst thing is not the airport automatic-flushing toilets. It's the little old ladies who piss all over the toilet seat because they're afraid to let the precious skin of their buttocks touch the same place where other buttocks have sat. I can just picture them hovering over the toilet seats like primordial insects spraying the area below.

In Japan, the toilets are just holes in the ground. It is natural to squat over them, and you never leave with piss spots on the backs of your thighs. The only problem with Japanese toilets is that they do not provide toilet paper. You have to buy your own. Well, it would be worth it to me.

After I finally get some new insurance forms I send Stanley off to the doctor. But when he comes back several days later, he storms through the house and says his blood pressure was high, and the more worried he got, the higher it got. He now has a systolic reading almost as high as Jose Canseco's weekly salary over a diastolic reading somewhere in the range of Ken Griffey Jr's weekly salary.

This worries me. If Stanley has high blood pressure, he could die. Of course, we don't have life insurance, but what worries me even more is that if Stanley was gone, I am not sure there is anyone else out there who would be willing to have sex with me, especially if they won't even make eye contact with me.

Regardless of this setback in our insurance pursuit, we decide to go out and get a breakfast with lots of mayonnaise, ham (for Stanley – I won't eat mammals), pancakes, maple syrup and butter. Eggs, too. Poochus Pilate, our ninety-pound black lab, hops in the back of the Bronco (which is also uninsured) and scratches his back on the inside of the tailgate, causing the vehicle to bounce up and down.

"Would you stop that?" Stanley and I both scream.

We go to a place we call "The Country Place" because we can never remember the real name. This place is probably not a good place to go because of certain politically-incorrect practises having to do with gays. But the host is a personable young man of African descent who always loves to see us and shakes our hands when we come for breakfast. Besides his road buddies, this is the closest thing Stanley has to a friend, and so we regularly dine at The Country Place. But today the place is packed. Every table in the non-smoking section is filled. There are plenty of empty seats in the smoking section. But I think we both would just as soon jab our own eyes out with toothpicks than sit in the smoking section. I've had my share of addictions, but I can't understand why anyone would bother to get hooked on something that doesn't even get you high. At least heroin doesn't give you bad breath.

When a table is finally ready for us, it is right next to – you guessed it – the smoking section, separated only by a cheap lattice construction. My throat begins to burn and my eyes water as the smoke from the people next to us snakes purposely through the lattice and directly toward my respiratory system. Stanley asks if he should visit their table and fart all over their scrambled eggs like Garagantua. No, I tell him, but I love him for offering. Finally, they grind their butts into an ashtray. Our food arrives.

While we're eating, Stanley shows me a picture of Prince Charles in the newspaper. The future King of England is wearing little visor-like glasses that make him look as if he recently arrived from another planet in a very distant galaxy. We decide not to worry about the health insurance, the world is sure to end soon anyway.

The Language of Sharks

Nothing in the room stirred. Surely, the other side of the bed was empty, but Joan opened her eyes to make absolutely sure. He was gone. She had known that he would be. And she was naked, which only confirmed the worst. The morning light cut through the crack in her curtains like a hacksaw.

The inside of Joan's head felt airy and dry. She dimly realized she had not yet reached the hangover stage. Underneath that small comfort was another dawning realization: that she was still somewhat drunk and the hangover would be a category five by the time it hit her.

She rolled over, saw the empty brown quart bottle of beer lying on the hardwood floor, and attempted to look at the watch on her wrist. Her arm was bare. Her hand crept over the small round table beside her bed. No watch.

She groaned. She'd loved that watch – a silver-link bracelet and a dark red oval face. Robert had given it to her three years ago for her twenty-fourth birthday. She never took it off, but now it was gone. Instant karma.

She struggled out of the bed. If she stayed in it now, she would start thinking. She would remember fragments from the night before. Baseball. Beer. The bar. The rum and cokes. Dancing. Falling. Coming home with her student. She needed to avoid thinking about this at all costs. She slipped on a large T-shirt and some shorts and staggered out of her room.

"Good morning," came a cheery trill from the dining room.

Joan walked through the hall and leaned against the doorway, looked at Karen, fresh and blond in the creamy morning light pouring through the sliding glass doors, and said, "Not really."

Karen laughed her pealing laughter that only rarely indicated a response to something genuinely humorous. Then she said, "You really look like hell."

Karen already had on thick dollops of mascara. She was eating Frosted Flakes in fastidious, concentrated bites. Joan hated to watch Karen eat even on a good day. She went to the refrigerator, pulled out a liter bottle of Coke and began to guzzle it.

"Did you and Sam have a good time last night?" Karen asked.

Joan didn't answer. Instead she stared at the top of Karen's head until Karen looked up and saw the hard, bloodshot, yet eloquent eyes.

"Let's just say he earned his A," Joan said.

"Oh," Karen said.

Joan sat down at the table with the bottle of Coke and two BC powders. She poured the powders down her throat and chased it with the Coke.

"I never saw anyone do that until I met you," Karen said.

"It's the only thing that works," Joan said.

The phone rang. Joan stared at Karen. Karen licked the milk from the back of her spoon, got up and answered.

"Hello-o-o," she said, cheerily. "Yes, she is. May I tell her who's calling?"

Then she handed the phone to Joan and mouthed, "It's Sam."

"Hi," Joan said. Karen exited gracefully.

"Hi."

Silence. She felt as if someone had placed a pillow over her face.

"Listen, I'm sorry about last night," he said. "I feel really bad. I hope you don't take this the wrong way, but I don't think we should go out again."

Joan nodded and then realized that he wouldn't hear a nod.

"Yes, you're right. It wasn't a good idea. So, I'll see you later," she said. She hung up and put her head down. She had liked him and been pleased when he asked her if she wanted to go to a baseball game with him and his friends. But then they'd all gone out to the bar and, as usual, she drank until the place closed down. Then they'd stopped at the store to buy one more beer. It didn't matter that she couldn't remember the rest. He remembered it.

Karen came back in the room, slipping a bright yellow parrot earring into the hole in her earlobe.

"What did he say?" Karen asked.

"That he doesn't want to see me again."

Karen was mercifully silent.

"How embarrassing," Joan said. She glanced at her bare wrist. She couldn't seem to keep anything.

After Karen left, Joan slid open the glass door to the back patio and went outside. The yard sloped down to a valley of poles and electrical wires. Two black crows perched in the wild pear tree and cawed at her as if she were trespassing. She collapsed into the plastic chair and ignored them, ignored the flat blue sky overhead and the thin, anemic clouds.

She wondered what Robert was doing now. Maybe she should have gone to Germany with him after all. Instead, she'd decided to go to graduate school so she could write a dissertation on "class consciousness in prime-time cop shows" and teach media classes to sophomores. Well, it beat working for a living. But now she thought of Robert, remembered bike riding with him along the boardwalk, stopping for pistachio ice cream, and feeling the scrape of his beard in the mornings. She'd given that up so that she could get drunk and sleep with some kid who thought he could impress her by playing old Elvis tapes. She hated Elvis. Always had – even when he was alive, especially when he was alive. Then after she gets drunk and does the kid, he has the nerve to tell her he doesn't want to see her again. Well, now she wouldn't have to pretend that she liked Elvis.

Friday afternoon she came home from class. Karen was lying on the couch reading her *Cosmo.*

"Did you see Sam?" Karen asked.

"He wasn't in class today. It's all right. We only have another week. He doesn't have to show up, just turn in his paper. I'll give him his A and never see him again," Joan said. She silently thanked the gods he'd done well on all his tests.

"What are you doing tonight?" Karen asked.

"I don't know," Joan said, stepping out of her shoes. "Watching *Miami Vice*, of course. Then whatever. Maybe I'll make an early night of it."

"Good. I'll make some popcorn."

Victor knew better than to come over before *Vice* was over. At 10:02 Joan heard his familiar rap on the door.

"I wonder who that could be?" Karen said.

"I wonder," Joan said in a flat voice.

Victor opened the door and stuck his head inside. Slightly balding with a watermelon belly, wearing a uniform from the garage he owned, Victor did not cut a particularly dashing figure, but he had a gleam in his eye that made Joan turn away and grin the first time she saw him, sitting on a barstool at her favorite hangout. A shot of tequila had arrived at her table within forty-five seconds of that first eye contact. They'd been friends ever since.

"Y'all gonna answer the door or just sit there?" he asked, his heavy footfalls crossing the wood floor.

"We knew you'd let yourself in," Joan said.

"I think I'll go read a book," Karen said. "Nighty night."

Victor had a Tall Boy in his hand. Joan reached for it and took a swig. It was cold and bitter in her throat. She drank hungrily.

"I got five more in the car," Victor said.

"I was planning on making an early night of it," Joan said.

"That's too bad. I was planning on going out on the water for stone crabs," Victor said. "The boat's down at the marina."

Joan stared at the television and pictured her bedroom with its borrowed furniture, its unread books on the bed, the very smallness of the room.

"All right, all right," Joan said. She could never resist Victor's adventures. He was her other life. He didn't go to college. He wasn't interested in Marxist theory and couldn't tell you what it was though he suspected it wasn't good, but he did have an exceedingly fast Corvette, a six-pack of beer and a vial of cocaine as magical as one of Mary's bottles of wedding wine.

"Then let's go," Victor said.

The car swallowed the road with a voracious appetite, and Joan felt the wind washing her clean. Clean of the guilt of Robert, living without her in Germany, clean of the students and their smirks, clean of the professors and their bloody theories. If she heard one more feminist scholar natter on about vulvamorphism, she'd give up grad school and get a job at Hooter's.

She leaned over and kissed Victor on the cheek.

"What's that for?" he asked. Joan almost never kissed him, and if she'd ever had sex with him she couldn't remember it.

"That was so you'd give me a burst," she said and smiled wickedly at him. Joan thought she would probably like the comfort of his company even without the drug, but she wouldn't have denied that his bottomless vial added a certain zest to their times together.

"Let the games begin," Victor said, pulling out the vial from his shirt pocket. He rolled up the windows, and she took the tiny spoon, dipped it into the vial and then fit it carefully and snugly into her nostril. In a few seconds the drip hit her throat and an effervescent numbness crept down to the tip of her tongue. James Brown warbled inside her skull. She felt good.

Out on the black Gulf water, they skimmed the surface in Victor's new Boston Whaler. Sky and water melted together at the horizon. No one else she knew did this. Her university friends partied some, but their lives seemed thin and circular, orbiting around their classes and vocabularies. Joan didn't know what she was looking for, but sometimes like tonight she felt the answer bumping against the back of her head.

"Are there sharks out here?" Joan asked when he slowed down.

"Sure," Victor said. "There are sharks everywhere."

He pulled the boat up to a buoy.

"Come here and help me with this thing," he said. Joan leaned over and helped him pull the crab trap from the depths of the water up to the side of the boat and dump the crabs into a bucket. Victor shined a flashlight onto them. The crabs were pale gold with black trim. They waved big, meaty claws angrily at their captors. Victor had five traps. They stopped at all five and brought in seventeen crabs. One of the traps was empty. Victor said he suspected thievery. At the last trap, Joan saw a fin slicing the surface.

"Shark," she said.

"Yeah, a little one," Victor said. He tossed a crab out into the water near the fin, but nothing happened. Joan had just had another burst from Victor's vial and her heart spun like a music-box ballerina inside her ribcage. All her pores opened to the night air. Her lower jaw wiggled until she forced it still.

"Here let me try," she said. She threw a crab as far as she could toward the dark triangle. In a moment they heard a thrash, the water was thrown back like sheets from a bed. "He got it."

She fed the shark another crab and another, laughing. Victor watched her like a father who has given his child a new toy.

After three more crabs, the fin moved away. Joan watched until it disappeared.

"Guess he isn't hungry anymore," Victor said, reaching for the throttle.

"Guess not," Joan said. She settled back down into the boat, and drank another beer. She absently let her fingers scrape against the water and thought about sharks and crabs and the way the stars inhaled and exhaled the universe.

Summer arrived and put a hot, wet choke-hold on the sleepy college town. Emptied of a third of its population, the place acquired the surrealistic feel of a dissolving dream.

Joan didn't have to teach that summer. Instead she took some independent study hours and spent her time revising a paper about soap-opera semiotics to submit to a popular-culture journal. Every weekend she and Victor rode in his car down long desolate roads into the surrounding rural vicinities. They stopped at small white wooden churches, swam in sink holes on Saturday mornings to kill their hangovers with the shock of the freezing water, went night fishing for cobia, water-skiing on the lake or out into the woods to shoot his semi-automatic. All of it in the crystalline sharpness of his seemingly infinite supply of "treat."

"What does Victor's wife say about all this?" Karen asked Joan one evening as they were making a salad together.

Joan shrugged and cut into the flesh of a ripe tomato.

"I guess she doesn't care. I don't know. We don't have sex," she said. "We just like to spend time together." She dumped the tomato into the bowl and reached for a cucumber.

"I don't get it," Karen said, washing off the Romaine. "What can the two of you possibly have in common?"

"I don't know," Joan said. "It's just that he doesn't expect anything from me." She realized how shallow she sounded. Victor just liked her. She didn't know why he did, but she liked being liked that way. Maybe he even loved her a little bit. Never love them as much as they love you, her mother had warned her. You have to give if you want to get, her father had countered. But give what?

One night about midnight, Joan and Victor sat on a dock at a state park, overlooking a lake so dark it looked as if it had no bottom. They always gravitated toward water. Above them the moon shined a bright Cheshire cat grin. Victor skimmed his bottle cap over the surface of the water and then turned and looked at her.

"What's that scar on your eyebrow from?" Victor asked, pushing the hair from her face. Hardly anyone ever asked about that scar. When they did, she told them she got it in a bicycle accident.

"My dad did it."

"What'd he go and do that for?" Victor asked. His voice had a quizzical but non-judgmental quality.

"He was drunk, Victor. The man was a newspaper reporter. He was always drunk. My mom worked on the desk at the paper, so she was gone most nights, and Dad would take me to the bars with him. We'd watch football on the TVs or he'd give me quarters and let me feed the jukebox."

Joan leaned against a wooden post. Frogs sang from the shallows.

"So what happened?" Victor asked, bringing out the vial.

"I was fourteen when this happened," she said, touching the small white line that bisected her eyebrow. "We'd gone to the Coconut Tree, and there were some of his friends. They started teasing me. They were always giving me sips of their beers and trying to get me to sit on their laps."

"That sounds about right," Victor said. Joan lay down on the dock on her belly and scooped some of the lake water into her mouth. Then she spit it out at Victor, spraying his ear. Victor scooped a handful of water and returned the favor. She laughed, rolled over and stared at Orion's belt.

"This one friend of his, a reporter on the cop beat, always the sleaziest ones, starts kissing me on the neck. He's drunk, and I'm a little drunk, too because I've been taking sips of his beer and my dad's beer. So I don't even get it. I just let it happen. His hands start touching me. Daddy looks over and he goes ballistic. He knocks the guy off his barstool. This woman next to us screams, and the next thing I know, Daddy is dragging me out of the place by my hair. He's in a complete and total rage. I mean, he never was a violent drunk. Not until that night. We get home. He hasn't said a word, and then he just shoves my head right into the living room window. My mom comes home, finds me bleeding all over the carpet, he's passed out on the couch with the TV on. You can imagine. She left him the next day, and I didn't see him again until he was in a casket six years later."

She could still see his stiff face against the white satin pillow, a face that said absolutely nothing. A statement of utter absence. She tossed a stone into the black pool of water.

"I've been sinking ever since," she said, watching the ripple undulate across the surface. Victor didn't say anything but she felt his eyes pasted to her profile, so she finally turned to look at him.

"What happens when you reach bottom?" he asked.

"What?"

"You said you've been sinking ever since," he said, his head tilted, his eyes gazing at her as if he'd never seen her before.

Joan shrugged and thought of the stone descending through the dark layers of the lake.

"I guess when you hit bottom, there's nowhere to go

but up," she answered. Victor reached over and touched her bare toe.

When the phone rang at five in the morning, Joan jerked herself awake and answered it.

"Hey," she said, knowing that only someone halfway around the world would call at this ungodly hour.

"Hey yourself," Robert said. "Did I wake you up?"

"Yeah, but it's all right," she said. "How are you?"

"Fine, fine."

There was a pause, a long-distance urgency to say something meaningful. But in her sleep-addled brain, she couldn't think of anything.

"You could write once in a while," she finally said.

"I've never written a letter in my life," Robert said. Another pause. "Listen, I've got a question for you."

"What's that?"

"I need to know if I should be waiting around for you. I mean, when you get done with all this college crap, are we getting married or what?" he asked.

"It's not crap," she said.

"You know what I mean. For God's sake, how much education does any one person need?"

"I don't know, Robert," Joan said, wishing she hadn't woken up to answer the phone after all.

"You don't know what?" The darkness of the room leaned over her.

"I don't know anything," she said.

"See what I mean?" he said softly, sadly.

The fall semester arrived abruptly. The streets were flooded with new and returning students. Joan wanted to get out of town and forget about them, get away from their frat parties and sorority rushes, farewell hugs with their parents, lost expressions and blind enthusiasms. Her paper had been accepted, but she didn't care much. Friday night encroached, and an electric energy coursed through her.

Joan clipped her toenails on the couch while Karen got ready for her date that night. Karen wore a bright pink sweater, a pair of white slacks and white pumps. Two bright streaks of blush cut across her cheeks; her freshly highlighted hair bounced like the girls' in the commercials. At exactly seven-thirty, there was a knock on the door. Karen answered the door and let her date in. She curled a hand around the man's arm and introduced him. Joan waved.

"Are you going out tonight, sweetie?" Karen asked.

"I don't know. I should go to the university. Our department has a guest professor from Duke giving a paper tonight at the Introductory Faculty Forum," Joan said.

"Really? What on?" Karen asked.

"'Fear of the Vagina in the Films of John Ford'," Joan said. "I kind of like the alliteration, don't you?"

Karen's date shot her an alarmed look, and Karen's pink lips spread in a wide smile.

"Well, have fun," Karen said.

"You, too."

On *Miami Vice* Sonny Crocket drove off into an Art Deco sunset. A moment later Joan heard the familiar purr of Victor's 'vette in the driveway. She got up and looked in the mirror above the stereo. She wore a white blouse, black jean shorts and a shark tooth necklace that Victor had given her.

"Fits your personality," he'd said, and she took it as a compliment.

The doorbell rang; Victor opened the door before she got to it.

"Ready?" he asked.

"Sure," she said.

A tall blond man, handsome in a salesman kind of way, stood behind Victor.

"This is Ray, my best friend from back home," Victor said.

Ah, best friend. Victor would want to show him a good time.

"He sells boats," Victor said. Ray smiled. Yeah, she thought, he probably sells plenty of them.

As they walked back to the car, Victor told Ray with his usual hyperbole that Joan was a college professor.

"I am not," she said. "I'm a graduate assistant. I teach a couple of classes and take a couple."

"Yeah? What are you studying?" Ray asked. He opened the passenger door to the 'vette.

"Communications theory," Joan said. "How the hell are we all gonna fit in here?"

"You'll have sit on Ray's lap," Victor said, getting in the other side.

Ray slid into the passenger seat, and Joan squeezed in on his lap. She felt his jeans against the backs of her knees. The hair on his tan arms was golden. She'd always liked men's arms. She pushed her hair behind her ears and gazed at Victor.

"So have you got some theories about communication?" Ray asked her.

"One or two," she said as Victor handed her the vial.

"Treats for the queen of sharks," Victor said.

"Thank you." She took two healthy bursts and felt the white pebbles explode in the far reaches of her nasal cavity. She held the spoon for Ray as he snorted with expert marksmanship.

"Where are we going?" she asked.

"The coast," Victor said. "I borrowed a condo."

She felt Ray's hand snug around her hip, and then a

moment later Victor's hand slipped off the gear shift and onto her knee. In a moment of prescience, she saw the night ahead of her. She knew men, and she knew that where two or more are gathered together, they often lose their more human qualities. It would be easy enough to tell Victor to turn around now. That was the message they were sending, a friendly forewarning of the expectations. Not that it was planned this way. Not until the moment she had sat on Ray's lap had the outcome been decided. And then it wasn't even a decision. It was a groping toward the inevitable.

"Have you got anything to drink?" she asked.

Ray pulled a pint of Cuervo Gold from the back. She unscrewed the top and put the bottle to her lips. The tequila slid onto her tongue and raced into her belly. Joan understood the dialogue of muscles. She let hers unfurl. After a while, Ray's hand reached up and undid the top button of her blouse. Again she had the opportunity to alter the tone of the evening, to button it back, but she didn't. Victor's eyes recorded the loose button, but his facial expression didn't change. He continued talking about fiberglass boats and outboard engines and how fast you could go on flat water; Ray threw his line into the conversation periodically. Victor's fingers softly rubbed the inside of her knee. She didn't know what made her decide not to put on the brakes. She wasn't powerless here. Maybe she was just finishing something that started a long time ago.

She hung her head out the window and exposed the ribbed bones of her throat. She thought of a television show she'd seen recently where they made a nurse shark go docile by turning her over on her back. Another button from her blouse came undone. Victor's hand reached over and caressed her skin. She felt his wedding band. She looked at him. She noticed a tension in his jaw line as his eyes steadfastly searched the road in front of them. She heard a question in her mind: how much education does one person need?

"A lot," she said.

"What?" Ray asked.

"Nothing. Give me another drink."

They reached the coast in thirty minutes. Victor pulled his car into a parking space in front of the condos. Joan disentangled herself from Ray's legs and arms. She walked into the dark condo between the two men. She heard Ray shut the door behind her. It was a moment or two before Victor found the light switch.

Her student loan arrived the Friday after classes had begun. She finished teaching her class on Intro to Communications and took the check to her bank. Instead of depositing it, she cashed it.

She found her passport at the bottom of a suitcase. She hadn't used it since she'd gone to visit Robert one summer in Venezuela. He worked for a technology-development company, and so he traveled a lot. He had said he was tired of it and wanted to settle down somewhere for good. Karen stood in the doorway.

"I always wanted a man to call me and say, 'Wear your black dress and bring your passport'," Karen said. She had the strangest notions of the romantic. Joan put the passport into her purse, and started packing the suitcase.

"What about your classes?" Karen asked.

Joan imagined the confused look on the departmental secretary's face as students filed in and said their teacher hadn't shown up for class that day and she felt something akin to happiness. Then she wondered how long it would be before one of the students actually did raise questions. They could probably go the whole semester quite happily sitting in the classroom sleeping or reading their newspapers, but eventually someone would catch on.

"They'll figure it out," Joan said.

"Well, I envy you," Karen said. Joan looked into Karen's wistful eyes. Then she thought of that night in the condo: her nose an Antarctica of white powder as hands prodded at her flesh, knees pushed against hers, mouths excavated her body. In the light through the windows their flesh looked silver.

"You reach a point," Joan said, "when your needs become toxic."

"What?" Karen asked.

"Nothing," Joan said. "Will you drive me to the airport?"

Joan looked out the window as the wheels of the jet were tucked into its belly. She saw the ground expand and diminish at the same time. To the south, the flat blue water of the Gulf lay thick and smooth like melted wax. Across the ocean Robert slept in the night's shadowed heart. Joan reached for her throat and felt the shark's tooth that still hung on her neck. She remembered the next morning when Victor had taken her home. They'd left Ray back at the condo, still asleep. She and Victor didn't have much to say, but when they reached her driveway, Victor turned off the car and took her hand. I love you, he'd said. But all she had wanted to do at the time was to go inside and take a long, very hot shower. Now, running her finger across the tip of the sharp tooth, Joan realized that perhaps Victor had loved her. He'd taken her to the bottom, after all. She unclasped the necklace and held it in her palm a moment before dropping it into the ashtray and closing the metal lid with a click.

The green world dropped away and the jet lifted toward the wide sky.

Suburban Hunger

Lately I am very hungry at night before I go to bed. Last night at midnight I ate peanut butter on table water crackers, scooping the peanut butter out of the jar with the crackers. I don't know why I'm so hungry. For years I hardly ever ate peanut butter, but in the past few weeks, I've begun to devour it.

I played volleyball yesterday with my daughter and her friends. Maybe that's why I was so hungry. I am not a fat person. I also ate three carrots. I rarely eat carrots, but I've been hearing recently that raw food is better for you than cooked food. My best friend has cancer and she can't eat raw food. She takes a lot of oxycodone, so I don't think she cares one way or the other what she eats.

On top of my bookshelf is a picture of the sunset in Maui. We went there in January because my husband's company paid for the hotel room at a very nice resort. Stan had to work part of the time that we were there.

His company runs sports events. My husband hates his job.

Every night as soon as he gets home from work, Stan plays a war video game while watching the all-news channel on television. Sometimes I wonder what we're doing together, what am I doing with someone who wants to do absolutely nothing except sit on his couch, the computer growling at him on one side and the TV blathering on the other?

I am addicted to reading. I don't exactly read for pleasure. I read non-stop, a book a week. I rarely enjoy these books, but I am a book reviewer and I always need money. I also devour magazines the way that I have lately devoured peanut butter. I read at the table, I read in the bathroom, I sit on the couch downstairs and read. I feel as if I'm soaking my mind in words the way you soak your body in a hot bath. I like to read books about holy people. They are almost always celibate.

When we were on Maui, we went to watch the sunset at the beach. Like any paradisiacal place, sunsets are ritual there. Our daughter splashed in the water. People gathered along the beach, sitting on isolated pools of blanket and towel. A man stood out on the rocks and beat a drum as the sun did a slash and burn on the clouds before sizzling into the horizon. I had my camera but was almost out of film so I only got one picture – the one that is now on my bookshelf.

I was wearing the short flowered dress I had bought at the outdoor Maui market earlier that day. As soon as the sun set, Stan was ready to go eat. Actually, he was ready before it set, but he tolerates my need for ordinary pleasures. As we walked along the beach under the still light sky, I noticed a woman sitting on the sand. She had long silvery blond hair and she sat very erect, with a serene smile on her face. From what I could see she must have been in her fifties. She was the most beautiful woman I had ever seen.

"Look at that woman," I said, nudging my daughter, Emily. "Isn't she gorgeous?" Of course, Stan was yards ahead of us, like the steam engine of a recalcitrant freight train.

"Yes," Emily whispered. We passed the woman, and I'm afraid our stares were obvious. But she simply smiled. We hadn't gone another fifty feet, when I stopped Stan and said I needed to go back. Stan is not a patient man, and he certainly has no interest in talking to strangers, but he would have to deal with it this time. I wanted to go back and meet that woman, to see her up close, to see if she was as beautiful as she seemed from a distance, to see if she possessed some secret for living that I could glean. So I turned back with my daughter in tow. We backtracked across the still warm sand to the spot where we had seen her sitting. There was no one there.

My daughter's hair is golden brown, long and usually tangled. In it she wears a hair wrap around a tiny braid made of blue, white and black thread with a metal crescent moon dangling from the end. She's lanky and stunning. Her eyes are shaped like softly-rounded rectangles and it's difficult not to stare at her eyes when she's talking to you. I try to make her wash that mane of hair once a week.

When I was little, my hair was darker than hers is, and it hung to my waist. My mother's friends called me "Lolita." I wonder why they said that. Was my need so evident even then in the midst of my innocence? I can't imagine anyone saying that about my daughter. For one thing, I wouldn't take it well. But, except for the hair, she's not anything like I was. I was angry and dishonest and wild. I played with boys. I loved the tussle and the hard pull of my breath as I ran from a petty bit of vandalism or pedaled my bike through the city with the gang. My girl plays in the woods behind our house, loves cats and has a battalion of girlfriends. She's dutiful about homework and never swears though she hears my foul mouth all the time. Emily has never stolen anything in her life. I was an accomplished shoplifter at her age.

Every morning I turn on my computer and work on various things – press releases for my clients, book reviews, whatever – but mostly I do email. I'll be working on something and the computer will stop and clear its throat, and then a little white envelope pops up in the corner. I always check it right away. Sometimes it will be an update from my best friend's mother on the progress of the chemotherapy treatments or missives from my cousin Todd about his sad state of affairs. But usually it's nothing – just some anonymous person with a name like Jackie or Meredith wanting to show me pictures of singles in my area or trying to sell me Valium or Viagra over the internet.

I live in a suburban neighborhood where everyone drives an SUV or a mini-van. A few do drive sedans – Toyotas or Hondas. And one blond woman in her fifties drives a red convertible. I drive a Ford Escort station-wagon. The seat belts are held together by duct tape because a stray dog chewed through all four sets of shoulder straps when I was trying to find a home for it.

The houses in our neighborhood have big yards with perfectly maintained lawns. These houses were built in that weird time period when developers never put in sidewalks. Nowadays they build the houses all crowded together, and there are sidewalks on one side of the road. But our neighborhood was built about twelve years ago, a pioneer encampment of future sprawl. I call it the historic district because just about everything else around here was built last week.

Yesterday I walked over to the house where my daughter was playing volleyball. Since we don't have sidewalks, I walked along the white curb. Worms lay dried up on the concrete and looked like something you would see in chow mein. One worm was still alive. I picked it up, much to its annoyance, and tossed into the grass.

The women in this neighborhood don't like me. They don't hate me either. It's just that they knew from the moment we moved here that I wasn't one of them. Like in college, no one would have dreamed of asking me to rush for a sorority. I just wasn't the type.

I have observed that having too many friends is a major pain in the ass. They always want you to do things with them or for them. They give you presents for your birthday and then you have to remember their birthdays. Or they get cancer and break your friggin' heart.

There is one woman in the neighborhood who does seem to tolerate me. She is a high school science teacher. One person is all I need, and I wouldn't exactly say that I need her. We take walks together every other morning and I tell her what I've been reading. She doesn't seem particularly interested. Then she tells me about her family which is flung all over the globe. She is German. Having her for a friend is not particularly demanding.

Maybe that's also why I'm married to Stan. He doesn't require much maintenance. Hell, he doesn't require any. But taking him out in public is a tough call. Last week we had to go to our daughter's ballet recital. At the ballet recital, the director of the school stood on the stage in front of the microphone as if she were hosting the Oscars. She began to tell stories and stammer on about working with the kids and how wonderful they are. Then she talked about seeing a little girl with a walker and how sad she was when she realized that child would never get to dance. The story meandered pointlessly, and my husband kept saying in a not-so-quiet voice, "Why don't you just shut up and let's get on with the damn show." I had to elbow him lest other parents hear him, but it didn't do much good. He sighed and rolled his eyes and groaned. He refuses to play the game. I don't take the game seriously but, for crying out loud, I can play when I have to. The worst is when he has to find something in which to spit his tobacco.

I do not have what you would call a happy marriage. Then again it isn't a miserable one either. Not like my cousin Todd, who has not had sex with his wife in nine years – not since their third child was conceived. Todd tells me that he wants to get a divorce but there are the kids to consider and the fact that his wife would surely suck their bank accounts dry even if she won't suck anything else, and Todd is not particularly rich. In fact, he is not rich at all.

Stan and I do have sex once in a while, but we don't sleep in the same bed – or even the same room. This is one of the blessings of our marriage. I have discovered that it is virtually impossible for me to sleep with someone else, even the cat, in my bed. And when the other person snores at a billion decibels, I don't even have to pretend. Stan doesn't care. He makes his dog sleep with him.

I could describe Stan to you in two ways – one way you might think I was the luckiest old gal in the world, and the other way you would want to get me to a shrink immediately to find out why I live with this man. Even I'm not exactly sure why I live with a bigoted right-wing Republican when I am the kind of person I am, which is not bigoted (I hope) and definitely not a right-wing Republican. Not even a Republican, not even a moderate

Democrat. Truth is I vote Democrat or Green Party when that's an option, but I hate politics. I see the whole enterprise as ego-driven and generally fruitless, based on conflict and divisiveness. And though I don't care for either of those latter attributes, you could find plenty of conflict and divisiveness within the bounds of this matrimonial boxing match.

First of all, let me tell you, I'm not the kind of person to be in a relationship with a guy who has an old-man-name like Stan. I'm sort of a "Mike" kind of woman. There have been three major Mikes in my life and a few minor ones. There have also been a Kyle, John, Peter and Sam. But it's the Mikes I remember with the most fondness.

Stan is a bigot, yes. He is not the kind of bigot that I fear, however. He's the kind of bigot I pity. He does not like "black culture" – the songs and clothing styles that assault his tender white sensibilities from the television screen. Really, it is youth culture, but he can only see it as black, as different, as other. I know for a fact that in his own youth, he liked Motown. But he won't admit that to you now. He also will say disparaging things about other ethnic groups, but I do not allow him to use the "n" word. And he is not allowed to spew his ugliness around our kid. Fortunately, race is not an obsession with him so the times I have to hear that garbage are relatively rare.

Stan also thinks that homosexuality is immoral. This is a man who told me he once watched a woman have sex with a donkey in a live sex show in Mexico. (I'm not sure whether I believe that.) I tell him he's fucking crazy. Love is love is love. It doesn't matter the gender. So I send our kid to a school run by an out-of-the-closet lesbian. I figure that's all the antidote I need to his bizarre notions.

Most of the time I just ignore the bigotry. I figure he's

totally insane and as long as he doesn't act on his notions or infect our kid, and as long as I can tell him to *shut the fuck up!* once in a while, I put up with it. The fact that we are together still surprises me, but to tell you the truth, I have been around plenty of men who thought the "politically correct" way or at least the way I think. And they have often turned out to be unable or unwilling to apply their humanitarian principles in the home. You know what I mean? They'll scream at you or kick in the door or beat the wall. Try telling one of those self-righteous assholes to shut the fuck up. You'll be licking your own blood from your teeth. I've seen it. Don't tell me I don't know what I'm talking about. Hell, my dad was one of them – he played percussion with his musician pals whom he called "cats." He was one of those guys who thought we should abolish all borders between countries. You'd have to be a bonafide card-carrying commie to be more left-wing than my old man. But he didn't think twice about getting drunk and screwing some woman in the neighborhood and then slapping my mom in the chops if she didn't like it.

I'm sure there are guys who can be compassionate in the home as well as outside the home. I've even met a few of these guys, but I've never been in the right place at the right time, and so I've got Stan.

Besides, Stan has good qualities. One of them is that he cooks. And he cooks really well. He can grill up some shrimp kebabs or concoct a cherry pie without even a recipe. He can also fix just about anything that goes wrong with the computer. The most important thing about Stan is that he makes me laugh.

One day we went over to Fort Bragg to see the Air Show. He gets all choked up when he thinks about our boys (he never mentions the girls) in uniform who put their lives on the line so we can sleep snug in our little beds at night. On the way home, we passed a sign for a new development near the base. It was called "Bayonet at Puppy Creek."

"Bayonet at Puppy Creek?" I said, incredulously. Stan and I traded a glance.

"Well, it's a military thing," he said. "They like tough names. Bayonet at Puppy Creek. Slit Your Throat at Baby Crossing. Hand Grenade at Sweet Water." For days I imagined owning a new home in Slit Your Throat at Baby Crossing.

Another time when our kid mentioned that one of her classmates' last name was Biggins, he raised his eyebrows and said, "I'd hate to be a girl and have the last name of Biggins. Might be too much to live up to." I fell apart.

In our neighborhood all the women get together once in a while for parties that are not really parties. Rather they are opportunities to buy expensive kitchen gadgets or scrap-book kits or stamps to make decorative little cards. I always had an excuse not to go until finally about a month ago when I had a few extra dollars in the checking account, I decided to succumb. The conversation revolved around haircuts, French manicures, window treatments, granite kitchen counters, supermarkets and schools, of course. They drank and cackled and examined the merchandise. It was cozy enough, and I felt my mind slip free of its moorings. At one point, someone brought a baby over, and they all took turns holding the baby like they took turns with the pasta washer. I did not hold the baby. I don't have much interest in holding someone else's baby. When I had a baby, she didn't want to be held by anyone else. I like to see babies, but after a few minutes I'm ready to move on to something else.

Maybe I'm complacent. My life used to be different. I had lots of friends. I had lovers (before I got married anyway). I did things like go to movies and obscure little plays or poetry readings. But we have moved to the suburb of a big fat southern city. I don't need to go anywhere. I don't need friends. I have my kid and my computer, my books and magazines. But when I see my husband, his mouth hung open and his eyes glazed over as the computer says "Unit ready" for the millionth time, I rather expect the roof to come off the house and some force to pull me up and out like they say will happen in the rapture.

May is the month of hell for parents. After we'd been to the piano recital, the choral concert, the band concert, the ballet recital and the end-of-year ceremony at the school, we had one more thing to go to. Emily's school choir was invited to sing the national anthem at one of the baseball games played by the local minor league team.

I didn't grow up going to sporting events, but I always thought it would be nice to take my kid to one or two. I thought this would be more fun than chore. But Stan said, "I'm not going. I'm through going places. I work all day and I just want to come home and rest."

I tried to be sympathetic, but it's not exactly like he's working in the mines. Again I got that feeling that we were more roommates than married. But what could I do? Put a gun to his head? I wish I could say I was just disappointed that he wouldn't be there for our daughter, but the truth is that I wanted him to be there with me. The other things were obligation, but this seemed like it could almost pass for a date.

Emily and I left that night for the game before he got home. We went to the Taco Bell and got bean burritos for dinner and then we found the stadium. Once inside I dropped Emily off with the choir and wandered down to find the restroom. At the end of the upper level, a rock and roll band played one of the more popular – and better – songs that could be heard on the radio. I could see there was a woman singer but the voice sounded deeper than a woman's. It sounded surprisingly like the radio version.

After I stopped in the big wet bathroom, I wandered down to listen to the band. There were only a few people actually listening. I stopped and leaned against a rail. The woman began to sing "All Along the Watch Tower".

"There must be some kind of way out of here," she wailed. She had a great voice. Deep and resonant. And the musicians weren't bad – well, how good do you have to be? They sounded OK to me. I was glad then that Stan hadn't come after all because he wouldn't have wanted to stay and listen. The woman was blond and wore shorts. She had muscular runner's legs with a large tattoo of a dragon just above her ankle. Her hair was pulled back into a tight braid. I watched people walking by the band, parents with their children. They didn't even notice the band or the song they were singing. They were looking for restrooms, seating sections, popcorn and coke. They wore khaki shorts and seemed busy and intent. I wished Emily was with me so she could hear this woman sing.

The band played another song, one by Pearl Jam, and once again the woman pulled out all the stops with those vocal chords of hers.

"Thank you very much," she said into the microphone after the set was done to the five or six of us who listened and clapped. They were just the pre-game entertainment, but I thought that she saw herself in bigger and better places. I walked up to her as she bent down to unplug a cord. I caught her eye, and she stood up and turned around.

"That was an awesome Hendrix," I said. I knew she'd be able to tell by the silver strands in my dark hair that

Hendrix was my era. Not only my era, but my place in the universe. Of course, she wouldn't know that I had seen him in person when I was fourteen, but that didn't matter. What mattered is that in this place she would know who I was, and she would know that I knew who she was. We were members of the same tribe at some level. I was an ex-patriot, living in suburbia.

She took my hand. She wore purplish-white lipstick, and her eyes were like swords. "Thank you," she said, pumping my hand. "Thank you so much." And for an instant, I was a fan. I was one of those people who could follow another's aura of greatness and bathe in it whenever possible. I felt that the goddess had reached out and said, I haven't forgotten you. Perhaps I blushed.

I left her packing up the instruments and went to find my seat. The baseball players were warming up in the field, and to the west the sun was setting, leaving red claw marks against the deepening blue. I thought of the beautiful woman I saw in Maui. I thought of this rock singer with her dragon tattoo. I thought of the goddess. I was such a lost sheep.

I got home that night, ate a banana and some peanut butter and crackers and went to bed. In my dreams, Jimi Hendrix wore purple lipstick and sang "All Along the Watch Tower" while up in a cage, I danced in white go-go boots.